C000133831

EDDIE
& ALAN

First published by Indy Pub 2024

First edition

ISBN: 9798869139535

Cover art by Anthony Amiewalan
Editing by Julia King
Advisor: Mikael Schulz (Photography)
Advisor: Toby Childs (Beta Reader)

EDDIE & ALAN

A Novel

Anthony Amiewalan

This book is dedicated to the process we all must undergo to find inner peace.

Contents

Preface

When we are young, there is this tremendous freedom just to be. It is a fleeting privilege but a powerful one that allows us to manifest the fullness of our emotional spectrum. Over time, as we settle into the world, we slowly lose this innate ability as we submit to the dulling force of our surroundings. We emerge shaped by the will of family, culture, and society. In this reshaping, we forget how we shone before. The need for acceptance, fitting in, and conformity increases in importance. When left unchecked, it can have a devastating impact on our lives and the lives of those around us. The story of Eddie & Alan was written to shed light on this erosion.

Eddie and Alan is written in a first-person narrative style through the lens of two men who reflect on their past friendship. The first two chapters provide a backstory of their lives, and the chapters onward are split between the two characters' perspectives, recounting the build-up and fall of their relationship.

Through this method of storytelling, I seek to shed light on how two people can view the same series of events drastically differently and how that difference is made more pronounced by the lack of sharing of perspectives and simply communicating.

I explore various themes in this novel, including racial identity, sexuality, and trauma, by diving into the backstories of Eddie and Alan, and examining their anthologies manifested in their interactions with each other and the people in their lives.

The goal is to contextualize the actions of Eddie and Alan but also to show how their past informs how they show up in the world.

The story of Eddie and Alan is meant to serve as an allegory. It explores the results of what happens when emotions and feelings become the sole foundation of how we make decisions and how those decisions impact the way we perceive the world and ourselves.

Opening

I want someone I adore
  Someone who makes me feel sure
  I got a problem I always want more
  I wish it was like before

Before, before you
  Before, before I knew
  What boys can do to you
  I, I want it to feel like before...

Seinabo Sey, "Before," from the 2023 album *The One After Me*

1

Eddie

This pain is unbearable. I can't sleep most nights—my mind races. I miss him. I miss what we had, or what I thought we had. I think I loved him. Why can't I move on? After all, he didn't give me much to hold on to anyway. Yet, I'm here, waiting under the Brooklyn Bridge, lost in my thoughts about him.

The activity around me breaks my concentration. The sounds from honking horns, foreign languages, and ambient music temporarily distract me from my rumination, but not for long. I sip the hot cup of coffee in my hands, letting the black bitterness roll along my tongue to cool it, the flavor and smell penetrating both my taste buds and nostrils, before bringing the cup back down and placing it along my side on the bench. I allow myself to enjoy this momentary distraction. I sink into being off work, at midday, and a tourist myself. However, I only stay in this illusion for a short time. Today, March 20, 2023, marks the natural transition between winter and spring; ironically, I'm struggling to accept the recent change in my life.

For this reason, I'm hoping to speak to a psychic. Maybe she can give me insight into my future—for I need reassurance.

I thought the grass was greener on the other side, but my imagination betrayed me. Will I see Jacob, my boyfriend, again? Is this breakup temporary, or is it over? I need something, dear God, *something* to help ease the pain, the pain of loss. Palm Springs undid six years spent cultivating a relationship with Jacob, now withered away in only three days. I need to know that it wasn't in vain. I need the universe to show me a sign that this is just an anomaly, a wrinkle in time. In the end, everything will be ironed out and returned to the way it was: perfect.

My name is Edward Adenjj, but growing up, schoolkids called me Eddie. My cousins called me Red due to my rust-toned skin, which set me apart from the variation of beige I encountered at school—well, that and my hair. I have kinky hair, the characteristic zig-zag curl pattern typical of members within my race. I've gotten the hang of managing it, allowing its texture to stand and spread, hovering like a cloud.

Two months ago, I turned thirty. I am old enough to know better. Old enough not to put all my eggs into someone else's basket—especially someone that doesn't appreciate them, but I'm naïve. I deceived myself into believing that I was in love. I chose to blind myself to love's complexity and instead settle for the shell of its promise; I gave Alan everything, hoping he would validate me. Instead, I was given the pain of rejection. Oddly enough, that comforts me now—the pain. For the pain is all I have that feels real. It gives me strange comfort—a sense of peace. The pain grants me something to hold on to, to process and stew in as I wait. The funny thing is that I've never been good at waiting, although I managed to as it relates to this hologram of a relationship I had with this man for over three years. He gave me ample practice, and I accepted it. It took almost a year before my first kiss with Alan. We were at a coworker's going away party. With his hands still grasping my arms, Alan pulled me away from prying eyes, kissed me on the neck, grabbed my drink, finished it, and led me toward the exit. I waited a goddamn year for that moment, but when it actualized, it was easy for me to release control—to let go and allow his will to guide mine. I guess it's a force of habit. Allowing others to lead has always been a space I'm most comfortable occupying— that and doing my best to be respectable, "likable." I've always wanted to please, blend in—to be the perfect wallflower. Never too pushy or aggressive, but always accommodating.

***

From a young age, I learned the wisdom of lying low to avoid the impact of being hammered down by others. I think this philosophy was embedded early in life. I attended primarily white schools and stood out. How could I not? I am a gay black Nigerian boy with a funny last name. To compensate for this unasked-for exposure, I sought to be small, invisible to the eye. Physically, this manifested in my voice; I spoke in whispers. Symbolically, this showed up in how I expressed myself, or the lack of self-expression. My opinions were secret; I became an expert at mirroring others. My superpower was empathy; I morphed into the feelings of others, shapeshifting until I didn't recognize myself. I was comfortable there, used to this guiding blueprint that provided safety. I did not want to feel the force of someone else's hammer, so I complied, working in tandem with the expectations of others to remain flush and surface.

I was born January 24, 1993, in New Orleans but grew up in a small town in Iowa, located on the western side of the state, which had no more than ten thousand people. Most of the residents were of German descent. It was a typical small

Midwestern town—American flags hung waving on residential porches and on poles outside local businesses. The courthouse anchored downtown, which was centered in the middle of the city; from it sprung Main Street, flanked by an assortment of shops and restaurants on both sides. It was an idealistic setting. I appreciated the variety of offerings, from the local diners to specialty stores, my favorite comic bookstore, and the old theater—where you could watch a movie for a buck fifty.

My family and I adjusted to life in a small town by following strict moral codes of conduct. We were a black family in a majority-white town. My parents were African immigrants, both having migrated from Nigeria to build a better life in the States. They were highly skilled immigrants, too, engineers who worked in local manufacturing plants. My father led the engineering team at his plant, and my mother was the only woman at hers. They carried the weight of being exceptional because of their circumstances and the burden living in the United States brought them as blacks.

I have a sister and a brother. They're fraternal twins, ten years younger than me. Unlike me, they've only known Iowa. They were born after we moved. For them, quiet suburban blocks and grand upper-middle-class homes were the norm. They knew what pop was (soda) and gleefully participated in the Fourth of July parades and cliquey neighborhood rituals of setting up lemonade stands.

After two years of living in Iowa, my parents built a pool in our backyard. It was an accomplishment, considering they were foreigners, ethnically and culturally, but somehow, they managed to achieve the American dream, which was validated by our neighborhood cosigning to their success. My siblings didn't bat an eye when entire families came to swim in our

4

pool. White bodies walking to and from the gates of our home didn't instill fear; no, they experienced comradery. This setting defined my siblings' childhood—for a time, they couldn't see how we were different.

However, unlike my siblings, I was painfully aware of my differences. We lived in Kenner, Louisiana, before moving to Iowa—a suburb of New Orleans located in Jefferson Parish. I have many fond memories of Kenner—some fantastical. One of them involved a pack of stray dogs. Yes, I encountered a group of wild dogs while running away from home. I was upset with my parents because they wouldn't buy me a PlayStation for my birthday, so I decided to run away to punish them. In my escape, I found myself in a concrete canal with grass growing sporadically through a series of cracks due to the lack of maintenance. Looking up from its pit, I saw two or maybe three dogs. Our eyes caught, locked in stillness for no more than ten seconds, and from there, the chase began. I escaped, leaving the canal, jumping on top of the first car I saw, and waiting them out before leaving the roof. When the coast was clear, I went home to my parents, thankful for them and the safety of our home despite their perceived unfair treatment.

Kenner was full of adventure. It was where I made my first best friend Kenji, a Japanese boy who had newly immigrated from Japan. We played Super Mario Brothers together, and he proudly displayed his Japanese Manga collection. We tried po' boys, ate pig's feet, and attended mardi gras celebrations together, sharing the spoils of beads and toys thrown by partygoers on the floats. We'd sneak into places together, too, like when we went to our neighbor's backyard party and helped ourselves to their traditional crawfish boil.

Living in New Orleans, we weren't strangers to extreme

storms. The streets and canals would often flood. Sometimes, we'd meet up and swim in the streets—laughing, unaware of the dangers and hardships these floods brought to the city. We were children, blissfully engaged in each other's world; he was my best friend, and I loved him.

We left New Orleans when I was ten. It was immediately after my mom gave birth to my siblings. My father received a job offer to lead a mechanical engineering team at a car plant near the town we moved to. After a year in Iowa, my mom found a position as an engineer at a manufacturing plant adjacent to my father's that created car parts. I mourned the loss of my Kenji and New Orleans. It took me the entire summer after arriving in Iowa to adjust to our new community and even more time to acclimate to my new school. Unfortunately for me, I could have made a better first impression.

I was a terrible reader. Once, while reading aloud in my now all-white school, I came across the word "Niger." I know it's a country in West Africa that neighbors Nigeria, but at the time, I was clueless. I couldn't distinguish it from "nigger." So, when asked to read aloud, I confidently said "nigger" instead of "Niger." Of course, the other kids, even the teacher, uproariously laughed. It was a humiliating experience that sparked my now lifelong struggle with shame. I had revealed my ignorance, felt less than, and since that moment, I tried my best to hide my failings and measure up. After that mishap, I committed to reading a book a month to improve my reading and comprehension.

At my new school, I searched for allies, friends, but found none. I tried earnestly to play with the kids during recess but couldn't connect. We didn't have the same experiences—I was different. This difference is perfectly seared into the memory of forgetting my lunch. My mother left work to bring me some food to eat. She'd made Jollof rice the night before and brought me some in a container. She'd made the dish with love, flavoring the long white grains with freshly chopped tomatoes, red peppers, onions, and other veggies and mixing in curry powder and red palm tomato paste, which enhanced the flavor and emitted the most delicious aromas. But, amongst my new companions, it embarrassed me. They joked about the strange smells emerging from the containers my mom had brought. I watched them, envying their perfectly cut sandwiches and packaged sweets. It was another indicator that my classmates keenly recognized that I didn't belong.

Despite my setbacks, I was determined to make a space for myself in my new environment. Hence, I devised a two-step approach to making friends. Step one was winning over my classmates, and step two was blending in, somehow making them forget my differences—fooling them into believing I was one of them. At ten, my only understanding of winning people over was through bribery. For a month, every day, I would bring bags of candy to the playground and hand them out. Chocolate was the favorite treat but the most expensive, so that happened four times and only on Fridays. The suckers with the gum inside (Blow Pops) were a close second. The third-tier candies were Jolly Ranchers and Tootsie Rolls. They were acceptable but not as prized.

To purchase the candy, I would use my weekly allowance. Ten dollars a week was given to me to allocate on activities or to save. I'd often consume the money on movies. I loved going to the movies. Or I'd buy comics. However, the mission to win over my classmates was critical. I disciplined myself and saved a portion of my allowance to invest in my bribery bounty for the entire spring of my first year. Midway through my confectionery-giving strategy, a classmate told me I didn't have to bring the treats in for people to like me, but I ignored her advice. She had friends; I thought she couldn't understand what it felt like to be me. I felt alone. I wanted to belong. She was right, though, and deep down, I knew it. Despite being presented with and knowing the truth, I put it aside. I effectively commenced developing and maintaining one-sided relationships where I identified a "need" and worked to fill it.

Pleasing others became my core; it inadvertently shaped my worldview, becoming the foundation of how I interacted with and felt comfortable around others. By age twelve, I started developing an awareness that my difference reached into my sexuality. Clarity came one day after gym class when my school conducted a scoliosis screening. We were asked to strip down to our underwear, line up in two rows on opposite sides of the room, and wait for the doctor to examine us. As we waited, I noticed the bodies of the other boys. At the time, I didn't understand why the feeling of seeing them exposed enticed me. I knew enough that this desire was different, unique only to me. So I pushed those feelings aside. I knew instinctively that if I explored them, they would lead to further isolation and rejection from not only my classmates but possibly my family.

The importance of blending in, being vigilant, and maintaining a respectable image was reinforced by my parents. This way of being was our shield, a way to ensure safety. But we had to do more than blend in. We needed to find areas of overlap where there was common ground between us and the community to build a foundation, a home. We discovered that commonality in our faith.

We were Catholic. We attended mass without fail every Sunday and regularly volunteered, donating both time and money. Every Saturday, twice a month, we would attend confession. Our parents valued this time with us because it reinforced their desire to bring us closer to God. We'd arrive at church shortly after noon, line up in a pew with the kneeler down, our eyes closed, and our hands clapped together, touching our noses in prayer, waiting to be seen by the priest. After the last of us received the sacrament, we'd bring out our rosaries and begin to say the Hail Mary chaplet together. My parents also wanted to ensure that we completed our penance, which usually consisted of five Hail Marys and an Our Father.

When I transitioned into high school, I did my best to stay ahead of the curve to conceal my sexuality. I didn't date. Luckily, most thought I wasn't interested in dating outside my race, and there was no option to date another black person. However, there was one curious white girl. She attended the other Catholic feeder school. Her friends attempted to get us together multiple times, but I managed to evade them each time. I explained that I had strict parents and wasn't allowed to date, or that I was too busy because of all the sports and extracurricular activities I participated in. Somehow it worked. I was left alone and allowed to exist outside the dating rituals baked into the prevalent high school ethos.

When the time came for me to leave high school and transition to college, the decision—driven by my parents—was that I would attend Iowa State's School of Engineering. It's almost compulsory for black children of African or Caribbean descent to attend college in a STEM field. After all, it usually requires sacrifices for the parents from these communities to get to the United States. They want their children to fully embrace the American Dream, which means being in careers that guarantee their success and place in life. I understood this contract; my parents didn't want me to be far from home. They wanted the ability to check on me and their investment to ensure that I stayed on track.

They visited me every other weekend, bringing Jollof rice and stories of my cousins and other children's successes amongst their Nigerian networks. These accounts were meant to motivate me to do and be better, but they only made me resent them. Inadvertently, they cast a constant cloud over me, saturated with feelings of inadequacy. I never felt good enough.

Halfway through my sophomore year, I decided to change to public policy and urban studies. It was just a better fit. I was competent in math and science, but my heart wasn't in it. I was merely going through the motions and following in the path of my parents. But public policy thrilled me. I'd always wondered why we had to drive an hour and a half from our home to get our haircuts; the same was true for my mother and sister to get their hair braided.

There were apparent differences between the community I lived in and the one we visited when we saw our barbers or beauticians. There was less diversity of shops and restaurants; it appeared that fast food places dominated along with liquor stores and churches. I asked my dad why on one of our many drives, and he shrugged. I always wanted to know the "why," to understand it and change it—to make a difference.

I told my parents I wanted to change my major over winter break. I broke the news to them after dinner during the second night of being home for a two-week vacation. While my brother and sister cleaned the kitchen, I pulled my parents aside to share my decision. It didn't go well. They couldn't see the point. A career outside the pre-approved and certified field of medicine, law, or engineering seemed outside the realm of reason. It wasn't a choice, but I dared to be different. I dared to be the nail that stood up above the rest, refusing to be hammered down.

My parents only came around after a discussion with my "uncle," a close family friend who had established his career working for the government in Iowa. He immigrated to the States before my parents and had a long stable job with the state that helped put his two kids through college. Now, newly retired, my uncle was enjoying his pension from his years of service. In retirement, he spent his time traveling back and forth between the U.S. and Nigeria, advising others who dreamed of immigrating to the States like my parents. His example and explanation of the benefits and security of working a government job set my parents' minds at ease. Two years later, I graduated with a major in public policy and a minor in urban studies.

After graduation, I had a government job lined up through one of my uncle's connections. It was with the Iowa State Department of Development, which administered programs that provided federal and state funding to local communities to address various economic development needs. I was tasked to work as a program manager for the Community Development Finance Program—a program designed to encourage entrepreneurship in underserved neighborhoods throughout the state, particularly among communities of color.

For a year, I focused on managing CBOs that provided economic development services in the region where I grew up. It was fulfilling work to uncover the networks of black and brown businesses scattered throughout the surrounding communities. I discovered their stories and the organizations that sought to help them. I felt like I was making a difference but missing out at the same time. You see, I'd never left hometown. I was staying in Des Moines and visited my parents every other weekend, who were an hour and fifteen minutes away, and I'd also never been in a relationship. I repressed my feelings towards men and, at the same time, avoided being in relationships with women. I was lonely. I wanted to be in a relationship but needed a push to force me outside the closet.

A month after my first anniversary at this job, I left and moved to New York City. My parents were confused by the decision. They'd hoped I'd start focusing on finding a girlfriend and getting married. I was the firstborn son. I had a responsibility to set an example for my siblings. Besides, this was the next stage in my life that they'd help me get to. Why was I leaving a stable job and starting again in a new city? Especially New York City! What was the draw? I gave little explanation other than I wanted to be challenged and continue my professional development in the largest city in the nation, where economic growth was occurring at world-class institutions. They never fully accepted my explanation, but after seeing my commitment they provided their support.

A conversation with a coworker sparked the inspiration to leave Iowa and head to New York. While grabbing coffee, he'd asked me, "What do you want for yourself in life? Where do you see yourself in the next ten years—with work and personally?" Initially, it seemed to me a peculiar line of questioning. I didn't know him well, so I gave him a generic response. "I see myself married with kids and in an executive director role with the agency."

I'd never processed my career or being in a relationship. I'd figured it would happen eventually. But with who? After all, I was gay. I knew this much. I knew I wouldn't have a traditional family with a wife and three kids like my father. The reality was that I couldn't avoid being the nail that stood out, and this terrified me. I would eventually have to accept my difference or live an unfulfilled life. I decided to choose the former. I moved to New York the following year.

***

The ringing sound of an ambulance breaks my reflection, bringing me back to the present under the Brooklyn Bridge. My coffee is now lukewarm. I grab the cup, raise it towards my mouth, and drink the remaining contents. Satisfied, I check my phone to see the time. It's 1:50 p.m., and my appointment with the psychic is at 2:00 p.m. Slowly, I stand, stretching my arms, allowing the blood to fill my extremities. I speed up the process with several deep breaths in and out; each time, I notice the condensed air push out, fading into the sky. Standing, I throw away the coffee cup and tighten my scarf. I look down on the bench one last time to ensure I grabbed everything and walk five minutes to my appointment.

2

Alan

I fucked up. I shouldn't have let it go this far. I mean, I like Eddie, but it was just getting overwhelming. I just wanted to have fun. Someone to hang out with, to travel with—I wanted a best friend. Eddie was my best friend. He got me. I felt like I could be myself around him and wanted him around. I didn't want the type of relationship he wanted from me. Sure, I led him on. I admit I fucked up, but I tried to break it off.

I'm no stranger to fucked-up shit. I'm generally at the center of it. I've never been good with keeping, let alone *maintaining*, relationships with friends or family. Romantically, I'm trash. Not for lack of trying. Relationships, for me, have always been the icing on the cake. You don't need the icing; it's just there for extra sweetness.

Still, I feel bad. I didn't want to end my friendship with Eddie, but he gave me no choice; like a rat cornered against the wall, I jumped. Eddie wanted a romantic relationship, and I didn't want that with him. I tried to tell him this, indirectly and directly, but he wouldn't accept the truth. Regardless, I never wanted to hurt Eddie; I cared about him too damn much. For the first time,

I experienced what it felt like to be affectionate with another man, which felt good.

I just want to forget this drama with Eddie and focus on what's ahead of me. Today, my friend David, a buddy of mine since high school, shared a job posting based in Colorado that pays six figures. I'm trying to focus on my application, but I can't. I feel fucked up by everything that's happened. My inbox has a response from Eddie, but I delete it. I can't handle the stress. I need to get this off my chest. It's bad enough I'm in this empty apartment. The bare white walls are suffocating. I feel like I'm in a prison cell. The only difference is that my toilet is in a separate room. I have to get out, maybe go to Prospect Park to surround myself with nature, trees, and blue sky to clear my head.

***

"Get your ass over here. Who told you that you could go to that party? You intentionally disobeyed me. I told you that you couldn't go, goddamn it. You told me that you were going to sleep over at Cody's. Do you think I'm a fool? That I wouldn't catch your ass? You really must think I'm stupid. Well, you're caught, buddy. You're in big trouble now. Wait until we get home. Boy, you're gonna get it!"

That's my dad. He doesn't usually get *this* upset; my mom is the one who's overly agitated and hysterical. But he's upset because I lied. That's the one thing he doesn't tolerate.

I told my dad I was sleeping over at my friend Cody's house; instead, I went to the party. It was a huge deal because last year the party was raided by the police for underage drinking and drug possession. The news spread like wildfire throughout the school and eventually reached all of the community's parents, including my dad. Over dinner, my dad told me to avoid David, the name of the kid who'd hosted the party. "David is troubled and will only get you into trouble." I disagreed, and I wasn't shy about it. I thought it was hypocritical of my dad. After all, I'm sure he and my mom did drugs and drank when they were younger, so why was I being restricted? Besides, I heard the party was epic and hated being left out.

So, a year later, my moment came. This time, David was planning another party at his family cabin north of town. I hatched a plan to go. As I said before, I hated missing out—and I wasn't about to be the only person excluded or lumped in with the outsiders at our school. My dad dropped me off at Cody's house on Friday at 7:00 p.m. My dad loosely knew David's dad because they went to the same high school—but they weren't close, or so I'd thought. Unlike my dad, David's dad was more relaxed. He trusted David's judgment. He knew that David drank and smoked, but he was okay with it as long as David didn't get into trouble or did it at home. I wished my dad was similar to David's father, who was open-minded and progressive. For my sake, David omitted to tell his parents that I wasn't allowed to go to the party. Cody and I left his house after 10:00 p.m.

I did not anticipate my dad texting Cody's dad to check in on us—but he did. My dad arrived at the party close to midnight. When he got there, we were all drinking. David's parents knew we were at the cabin, which was reasonably remote, but shared the address with my dad to avoid the police getting involved. My dad violently opened the door and everyone stared blankly as he stormed into the cabin. No police this time. Just my dad. This year, the climax of David's party was my dad and his threats of beating my ass. It was an unforgettable night. I was at the center! Ironically, I liked that my humiliation served to bond everyone. Especially, me and David who later became my best friend. I'd even received sympathy from a few of the girls there. When we got home, I received the ass beating of my life and was grounded for months, but I didn't care. I cared about being included, a part of the moment, and being liked.

By the way, I'm Alan Nowak. I was fifteen when that story happened, and now I'm twenty-seven. It's an example of my rebellious streak—I despised authority then and even more now. I have my uncle to thank for that. He was a self-proclaimed Marxist. From a young age, he inundated me with books, including Karl Marx's *Manifesto* and Leon Trotsky's *The Revolution Betrayed*, that opened my mind to capitalist systems of control. He and my readings taught me to question all control methods, mainly based on capitalism, which set up CEOs as oligarchs. CEOs with undeserved influence who control political systems through lobbying and public policy manipulation. I hate them and argued passionately with friends about why capitalism should be abolished. I admired self-determination and the stories of ordinary people who broke out of capitalistic systems to set their paths in life, leading to something new—more democratic. The desire to chart my path led to my future career promoting worker cooperatives. But before we go down that road, let me introduce my family.

I have two brothers, each two years apart. Ryan is the oldest, followed by Noah, then me. Ryan is the smartest among us and the most socially awkward. He spent most of his time alone in his room, playing video games or reading Japanese anime. I bonded with him through anime and joined him as he entered multiple Dance Dance Revolution (DDR) competitions. At his core, he's kind, quiet, and a high achiever. Noah is the opposite of Ryan. He liked to fight with his words and fists. I blame the latter trait on my mother, who was physically and verbally abusive. Her constant messaging to him was that he didn't measure up. She compared us and our achievements, which caused him to hate Ryan and me—we constantly fought. He didn't fight as much with Ryan, but I became his punching bag. Noah was a rebel too. Always getting in trouble—but in dumb ways. Like when he got arrested for starting a fight at the bar because he disagreed about sporting stats. Someone called the police, and he was arrested for underage drinking.

Besides Ryan, we sought the attention of our dad. He worked as a missionary doctor. He was on the road for a quarter of the year, seeing patients. He'd often leave during the summer and stay home for the fall, winter, and spring. Once all the boys left the house, and it was just my dad and mom, his trips became more frequent and extended. I didn't blame him for needing to get away—our mom was a bitch.

My mom worked as an English teacher at the local elementary school in town. She treated us the same as her students—as dependents that required strict monitoring to meet her contractual obligations as a mother in the public eye. She cared for us like we were a nine to five job. The state required her to ensure we and her students met specific "standards" to move to the next grade or stage in life. I always felt that mothering was a job she had to do but never wanted. She took care of our basic needs, but nothing more than that—however, she was quick to criticize.

I grew up seeing her constantly argue with my father. It was a vicious circle. She hated that he was never around, but when he was present, she found issues in everything he did, whether it was cutting the lawn, fixing things around the house, even lovemaking. She belittled him, and he took it. I have an ugly memory of my mom's insensitivity. It was during a rare time we ate together as a family. Typically, we were never in the same space at once. If we were, we often chose to eat apart. However, my father was between projects and decided to take a week off work. It was early spring; I was in middle school, possibly ten or eleven years old. My mom usually made dinner, but he offered to cook that night. I was excited to see what he'd make; he told me in the morning, driving me to school, that he was planning to go shopping for food to make a big meal for us. When I got home, I saw he'd gone grocery shopping and had started preparing the meal. He landed on making us a gourmet version of spaghetti and meatballs. The house smelled terrific; well-seasoned meats, tomato sauce, and cheese with buttery cuts of French bread saturated our home with a savory aroma. When he called us all to eat, the first thing my mother said was, "This is it? You decided to make this for your family; you couldn't attempt something more creative or complex. That's your lazy father, mediocre to his core—in bed and life. Would it kill you to try harder? For Christ's sake, we're your family, not those snot-nosed kids you abandon us for in Africa or wherever the fuck you run off to." He didn't say a word, he just ate looking down at his plate until he was finished while my mom continued to curse at him. I lost respect for my father and my mother that night.

Her wrath wasn't just directed at our father—she saw her kids as a direct reflection of her. Because of this, she was heavily involved in our academics. If we weren't achieving according to her standards, there were repercussions—verbal and physical attacks. Noah received the brunt of these attacks. I think that's why he was so abusive towards me; he needed someone else to feel the hurt and pain caused by the woman that denied him love.

I swore to myself that I wouldn't be like my father or be in a relationship with someone like my mother. I would break the cycle, take control, and build relationships on my terms. This perspective took hold in my first serious relationship in high school with a girl named Angie. She was blond, fragile, and thin. I liked that she was thin and often complimented her on it— I knew this acknowledgment fueled her desire to keep up her appearance. The control was validating. She liked me so much that she was willing to do what I wanted to keep me happy. This control extended to our sex life too.

I started watching porn at twelve years old. It began with David sharing his dad's porn magazines with me and later discovering the plethora of free porn sites online. I'd spend hours in my room searching for the good flicks to jack off to. I was particularly partial to verbal porn—the idea of a man telling women precisely what he wanted, how he wanted it, and for women to listen and perform excited me. I liked pain too, or rather to give pain.

I liked Angie's personality too. I could sense her smile on the other end when we talked on the phone. Her voice was light and airy, childlike in tone. Listening to her talk was like hearing a chirping bird singing its song with the rise and setting of the sun. As much as I wanted to establish control, I tried to look out for her—for she was my source of love. Unlike my mother, she made me feel important—she nurtured my body and soul.

At present, I realize that this was dark. I was a manipulative prick who had unhealthy relationships with women. Do I regret my behavior? Yes, it was fucked up. I was an asshole. I needed to exert myself and establish control because so much of my life felt out of control. I didn't want to give anyone the power to hurt me, so I beat them to it. I was a smart aleck in class, constantly arguing with the teacher to prove my point, and unfortunately, I was emotionally abusive to my girlfriend. I can see that now, and I'm sorry.

I believe I loved her, although I'm not sure if she felt loved by me. Like my mother, I showed love by withholding—only giving it intermittently. I would express interest in a rock band and happily watch her jump on the bandwagon, trying to learn more about them. I'd read a book, and she'd have read it the following week, or I'd feign interest in a cuisine, which she would then attempt to make for me. However, when I sensed her withdrawing from me or showing reluctance to do something I wanted, I would withhold affection. I'd ignore text messages or just be an ass to trip her up. She'd cry, telling me she loved me—and I'd forgive her. I liked having the upper hand, morally—again, it gave me a sense of control. Our relationship lasted off and on again for almost two years. Once we left high school, I broke up with Angie, who became the foundation of how I learned to treat women.

I left home to attend a prestigious southeastern university for college and wrote for the school's newspaper. It was my first taste of diversity, me a Polish-American white dude with light brown hair and ocean-blue eyes. I'd not so secretly always wanted to date an Asian or Latino girl, and thankfully got to experience a lot of sex during my time there. However, one relationship affected me. I dated a black girl; her name was Evelyn.

Unlike me, who majored in economics, Evelyn was a journalism major. She was the paper's editor, extraordinarily proficient, and an excellent conversationalist. I was intimidated by her at first and, at the same time, attracted to her. A few weeks into my joining the paper, we went out as a team, and after everyone else peeled away, we were the only two left. We fucked that night and continued to see each other for the second half of my junior semester. The relationship didn't last. I was unsatisfied sexually; she wasn't into BDSM, sex centered around dominance, submission, and control. It was starting to be the only thing that truly got me off. I'd tried to be more tender and kinder with Evelyn, but it ultimately didn't work. On top of that, I felt an imbalance in our level of achievement. I began to resent her for her success and my comparative mediocrity.

During my last year in college, I decided I wanted to pursue a career in government—my interest in policy that supported the development of worker cooperatives intensified in college. I thought I might be well suited for a career in government. I applied to a program that allowed new graduates to rotate amongst various New York City agencies. At the end of my rotation, I applied for a position at the New York City Urban Development Corporation.

***

I'm getting ready to go outside for my run now. It's forty-seven degrees, so I'm searching for my tights, long-sleeved running shirt, and gloves to stay warm. Rummaging through the pile of washed clothes, I find blue tights and long gray running shorts. I also uncover the white Heat Tech running shirt I wore yesterday. I pull the items out, search for a skull cap and socks, and head out the door. Like an earworm, the track of my first meeting with Eddie played throughout my preparation. I left my apartment, desperate for relief.

3

The Connection

Eddie impressed me the first time we met. He wasn't cocky but soft-spoken and professional—willing to share information. It was refreshing. I came across a lot of douchebags that were quick to list their accomplishments and let you know that they had the biggest dick in the room, but Eddie seemed more humble, open to listening instead of enamored by the sound of his own fucking voice.

Eddie worked on the special initiative team. His job was to help the supplier diversity unit find minority- and women-owned businesses to serve as subcontractors to larger construction. I found my dream job managing an educational program to support businesses interested in forming worker cooperatives and helping them to access resources, like capital, to grow their business operations. I was referred to Eddie by a colleague to speak with him about his program and learn from his experience with program management in general.

It wasn't a surprise that I instantly hit it off with him. Eddie had a good reputation around the office. He was well-liked, well-dressed, well-spoken, and he was black. In my life, I found that black men like this were typically celebrated, especially in a place like UDC. There's always a push for diversity, which is ultimately good but sucks when you're white and male. We're just not as exotic. White men are sometimes made to be the enemy, especially in government.

In high school, we had one black kid, and he was super popular. I'm talking about the class president, varsity basketball, and football. He was excellent in everything he did. He wasn't discriminated against, as far as I could see. I think his being black opened up a lot of doors. For Christ's sake, he went to Yale. I firmly believe that you can achieve anything regardless of who you are. Although, I don't necessarily say this out loud. A statement like that would likely offend someone. As a white man, I'm always in danger of being offensive. I'd imagine that one could say I'm not considering the precedent slavery has had on upward mobility. To that I would say I do—but it feels like society today is bending over backward to make up for this injustice, at least from my perspective. And white men today are paying for it.

My theories on race and upward mobility may be unpopular; however, the real enemy of ordinary, hardworking people is the capitalist system that oppresses us and only allows a few to enjoy resources that all should share. During my initial meeting with Eddie, I presented my perspective on the limitation of upward mobility in this country and in most capitalistic societies, and I appreciated his openness to hearing me out.

Besides work, we talked about our lives in general. If you're a New Yorker, you know the first question people will ask you is, "Where do you live?" Now, this is an important question because it says a lot about you and your socioeconomic status. If you say, "I live in Manhattan, in Murray Hill," then that means you are likely a straight conservative white male working in finance with a six-figure salary. If you say, "I live in Brooklyn, in Bushwick," then you're a hipster in an artistic field, potentially down for a conversation on alternative lifestyles. I could go on with these stereotypes—they're much like old tropes in high school movies with all the jocks, outcasts, and geeks relegated to insular communities. The fact is that you're immediately sized up by the first information shared in casual conversation.

Despite the pitfalls of classism, living in New York was like a series of tidal waves crashing into each other—building into a tsunami, hitting the coast. The sensation of the sheer force against you was unmistakable and long felt. I'm a glutton for pain, so every minute was euphoric, though the recovery time varied. Coping with the aftermath of the crashing waves from the city was an adjustment. I've experienced lots of highs and dealt with a lot of shit. When I first arrived, I lived with two friends from college. We were "friends," I guess, but highly competitive. I never felt at ease. One worked in finance and the other in tech whereas I was still completing my rotations. We had fun, but they'd always bring up money, bragging about how much they were making and insisting on going to the most expensive bars and restaurants. It was already a stretch for me to contribute a thousand dollars a month for rent in our Lower East Side apartment, especially on an internship wage of twenty dollars an hour, and they knew it.

So, I purposely didn't contribute to household items. Why the fuck should I? They were making way more than me; besides, I was doing something that contributed to the public good. Unlike them, my job and trajectory were mission-oriented. I felt no guilt in skipping out on buying toilet paper or cleaning supplies for the house. If they could afford Rag & Bone jeans, they could throw cash at fucking Windex and paper towels. I didn't realize it, but my "friends" started to resent me.

It all came to a head one weekend when my roommate, Ren, planned to host a small gathering at the apartment. He mentioned it to me earlier in the week, but I forgot. I was stressed out. That week, I organized a summit inviting worker cooperatives to brainstorm policies to help formation of cooperatives easier in New York State. It was a week of meetings where I had to be on all the time and I was exhausted. When I came home, I would grab a beer or drink some of the communal booze in the bar cart. I contributed to the liquor occasionally, granted less than my roommates, but I never thought it was an issue. They made more than me and so had more discretionary spending power. Besides, my contribution was bringing fun and keeping the conversation going.

However, it became a huge issue. The night of the party, Ren stormed into my room, asking what had happened to all the whiskey and gin he had bought. I immediately apologized; I let him know I had a rough week and drank some of his booze to take the edge off. Ren completely lost his shit. He unloaded on me about not contributing to the household and being a leech. I understand he was upset, but it was uncool of him to bring in our other roommate, Veer.

They both started berating me for not buying toilet paper, paper towels, or the food and drink I consumed. I'd lived with them for almost a year, and this had never come up. I thought there was an unspoken understanding. I tried to make my case; they made more than me, yet we all split the rent equally. It was only fair that they'd contribute more to the household expenses. Plus, I thought it was unfair for them to get upset now. Why were they bringing this up? I found that this was a recurring problem

26

I faced: being oblivious to how people felt toward me. In high school, I applied to be class president and lost. I remember sharing my frustration with my then girlfriend, Angie and her admitting that she and my group of friends didn't vote for me because they thought I was cocky enough. It hurt my feelings then, but I played it off.

Similarly, my roommates hurt my feelings. I tried to do better in the future, that is, by being more observant of the emotions of others, but it has never come naturally to me. There was no need to share all these details with Eddie. When he asked where I lived during that first meeting, I only told him that I rented an apartment in the Lower East Side with two roommates. However, eventual I did. However, eventually, I did. I would share everything with Eddie. No topics were off the table. He would become my closest friend, someone to process parts of me unresolved. With Eddie, I explored my childhood, my dysfunctional relationship with women, my hopes and dreams, and my failures - parts of myself that I'd never felt uncomfortable sharing. I never thought he would hurt me. Besides, I loved that he was from Brooklyn. I was planning to move there, and he became another reason to do so.

***

When I first met Alan, he seemed extremely confident. A colleague asked me to meet with him to share advice on managing his vendors and providing the overall basics for program development. Alan was smart but was all over the place with his ideas and unrealistic standards. This naivety was understandable because this was his first full-time job out of college, and I don't think he understood the fine details of working in government. Before meeting with him, his supervisor shared that she was having trouble reining him in and keeping him focused on practical goals. Instead, Alan wanted to build a mass network of worker cooperatives and say that he did it; he wanted instant success. This zeal often happens when you start in government or a nonprofit; you set out to change the world but quickly realize the limitation on your goodwill. Red tape, limited resources, and misunderstanding of community needs can quickly contort your efforts. It is essential to approach the work with humility, with open ears, ready to adjust to the community's will with a watchful eye on political currents.

Alan was handsome. He had clear turquoise-blue eyes, as bright as I imagine the waters of the Caribbean would be. The center, in contrast, was saturated in black, almost as black as coal. He had light brown hair, which was likely originally blond but transitioned into brown as he entered adolescence. He had a patchwork of facial hair along his jaw and neck, which strangely added and subtracted from his overall looks. There was something unkempt about his appearance. He wore a gray suit flecked with blue and a light blue shirt. He was a stylish guy who clearly cared about how he looked.

We greeted each other at the door, shook hands, and as I took my seat in the empty glass-walled conference room, he closed the door and began talking right away. He shared the name of his program, the goals and outcomes he wanted to accomplish, and the associated timelines tied to each outcome. He then started to share anecdotes related to the work of the vendors he managed and wins he already saw with new worker cooperatives forming—because of his aggressive management. After that, he talked about his overall vision for the program and how that vision fit into his worldview: to create a more democratic workforce where employees' rights were expanded and shared more deeply in owner profits. He would look closely at me to ensure agreement between breaths and allow me to share feedback between water breaks. It was a one-sided conversation. I quickly realized he held very little interest in my work but needed someone to validate him and his ideas, which I was accustomed to doing with colleagues—being a sounding board instead of generating novel ideas.

The conversation moved from work to our personal lives. I'd moved to New York two years before Alan, landing in Crown Heights, Brooklyn. I worked at a small nonprofit based in Fort Greene, where I met my now partner, Jacob. Before starting at UDC, Jacob and I decided to move in together at his apartment in Prospect Heights, right off Vanderbilt, leading up to Grand Army Plaza and Prospect Park. My living near Prospect Park piqued Alan's interest. He'd visited the park with friends that summer and fell in love with the way it was less touristy than Central Park. Alan followed up with questions about the park and the neighborhood—how the nightlife was, if I went to the free concert series in the park, and about crime. He didn't ask much about Jacob, but I wasn't surprised. I find that straight men are typically wary of prying too much into the affairs of gay men. They want to show that they're down, but for them, it's a slippery slope to inquire too deeply into our lives, as though by showing interest they'll inadvertently diminish their masculinity. To combat that, I find that straight men either ignore discussion around sexuality entirely or engage while constantly letting you know that they are "not gay, no homo."

An hour had passed when we ended our meeting. Alan thanked me for taking the time to speak with him and asked if we could meet regularly so that he could bounce ideas off me and get my feedback. I said yes. Immediately, when I returned to my desk and logged into my computer, an alert popped up in my Outlook account. I received an email calendar invite for a weekly coffee meeting for the remainder of the year.

Buried under Alan's facade of confidence was pain. Our coffees revealed what was hidden under the surface, which was a longing for connection. I discovered that, like me, he was flawed. He had an uneasy relationship with his parents and siblings and the handful of friends he'd established thus far. During coffee, I created a space for him to share. I was almost like his therapist. We'd start our conversation about work and then move into other areas in his life. When it came to his relationships, I was initially disturbed by his views and experiences with women, but I didn't criticize him. I tried to help him see their perspective and how his actions impacted them. I shared my lesson in empathy with him, coaching him on what to say and why it mattered. I'm unsure how effective I was, but I saw that he listened, which flattered me. Alan was seeking me out for help. I was considered valuable in his eyes, and I loved that feeling.

4

Coffee

When I met Eddie, I was at a low point at work. My boss, Nia, and I clashed repeatedly. I often didn't agree with her or her approach to running my program. She was a micromanager, consistently inserting herself into areas that impacted the work I was hired to perform. Within months, I knew it wasn't a personality match. I resented her constant need to throw her title around and the many times she'd castrated me in front of the vendors I was responsible for managing.

The shit hit the fan during one of our check-ins. My lunch schedule varied—I rarely stayed within one hour. Nia scheduled a meeting at 1:00 p.m., which I missed. I was training for a half marathon that day and ran longer than expected. I left at noon and returned to the office a little after 2:00 p.m. I apologized, but she made a lot out of it. After that incident, Nia started tracking every issue she had with me. I felt like I was in a pressure cooker, ready to burst with my hatred for her. Well, I did explode. I asked her to stop riding me and to give me space to do my job. Ha. I said, "Get off my jock!" Like in high school, I was called into HR and put on a performance improvement plan. Word spread that

I was "difficult" to work with. So, when I met Eddie, I needed an ally at work. Eddie seemed calm, relaxed—non-judgmental. I jumped at the chance to get to know him and get his advice on navigating my boss and work politics.

***

From 3:00 to 4:00 p.m. every Wednesday, Alan and I would grab a coffee. The places differed. Sometimes we'd go to R&R, a mom-and-pop coffee shop with fresh pastries made in-house. Other times, we'd get a coffee to go and walk to the Seaport District towards Pier 16 and sit on a bench with views facing Brooklyn across the East River. I sensed Alan's loneliness. It was no secret that he was dealing with disciplinary issues. He had the reputation of being a know-it-all, unwilling to receive feedback, especially from women. He'd often talked over others during group meetings, and his manager received input from his vendors that his expectations could have been more realistic.

Despite what people said about Alan, I had a soft spot for him. Each time we met, he would open up more and earnestly ask for advice on how to improve, unlike when we'd initially met. At that time, Alan was not speaking to me but at me—enamored by the sound of his voice. Yet, over time, we transitioned into a conversation in which he actively listened to me. Alan was aware of his less-than-stellar reputation and wanted to change it. During our sessions, I'd explain how I managed my vendors toward success, meeting them where they were and joining in service delivery. I'd often say, "You must put skin in the game." Alan thought his job was to give orders and have people strictly execute them, but management is far more than that—you must understand people, their motivation, and how they like to work to achieve successful outcomes.

But, if I'm honest with myself, my intentions to meet with Alan weren't entirely altruistic. I found him attractive. Alan was a well-built, self-confident white man who sought me out for comfort and support. It felt good to have him need me, respect my opinion, and desire my company. I was rarely on the receiving end of this dynamic. I was usually chasing—striving to gain the approval of white people, particularly white men, but I never felt like I was the prize. It harkens back to my childhood, that is, the need to blend in and assimilate and gain acceptance from others. In my adult life this has manifested to a lesser extent in my romantic life.

I started to explore my sexuality at twenty-four, during my first year living in Brooklyn. Before moving, I worked with a realtor to find a place to live. I found a studio apartment in Brooklyn Heights for $1600 a month, a far cry from what I was used to paying in Des Moines. My rent there was $700 a month. I immediately found a job with a nonprofit in Downtown Brooklyn that provided business improvement and support services within the downtown commercial corridor.

Once I was settled, I decided to come out. The decision was fast-tracked, thanks to my first sexual encounter with a guy named Patrick. We met on Grindr. I was keenly aware of dating apps but hadn't created a profile until then. Patrick was the first person that caught my attention—a muscular, masculine-looking guy. I messaged him first; he replied, asking for nude photos. I complied, taking a few in the bathroom. Immediately after sending them, he asked if I was willing to travel. I said yes. In less than thirty minutes, we met at his hotel room. Mechanics took over my body as we kissed, felt each other up, and eventually had sex. I bottomed. I was afraid it would hurt, but he eased into it—taking his time, talking me through the experience, ensuring that I received pleasure. We finished, cleaned up, shared a few words, and then I was off, back to my apartment. A series of other encounters followed, all varying in intensity and seriousness. More one-night stands, casual dates, and dates that developed into friendships or friends with benefits; and, eventually, a full-blown relationship.

I was an addict. That first experience left me wanting more. I plunged into dating apps, allowing them to consume all my free time—even peeking at them during working hours. However, I uncovered an ugly truth about using dating apps as a gay black man—there's an unspoken and, in some cases, spoken hierarchy. I was open to dating various men as long as they fit within a specific gender expression and body type. There were lots of gay men who abided by this act of exclusion and had even further obstacles to elicit responses from the cream of the crop. You'd see profiles read "no Fems," "no Asians," and "no Blacks." Outward acts of prejudice and discrimination had no filter in the virtual world. I often heard the statement, "You're attractive for a black guy," from the predominantly white men I tried to court. Retrospectively, reflecting on my initial attempts to date, a sense of shame sweeps over me, but all I can do is give myself grace. Gay culture universally conditions men to put masculine gay white men on a pedestal via media representation and the overall celebration of Western beauty standards, similar to how white women are exalted, at least in an American context. It doesn't help that I'm an active consumer of porn saturated with images of white muscled bodies as the primary objects of desire. Porn, in combination with growing up in all-white schools, where my only crushes were straight white boys, all added to a warped sense of identity, self-worth, attractiveness, and a desire to be liked by white men. Plus, I was coming out. Self-love and self-esteem were concepts—not standard practices.

The last leg of my journey was to come out to my family. Six months after I settled in New York, I flew home to celebrate Thanksgiving. My parents would often call every week to check in about the move, work, and my personal life. They were both eager for me to start dating and eventually marry. My mom would tell me stories of my relatives and their family friends who were either engaged or starting to have children. She'd say that I was still young, but it was best to begin the process of dating, preferably a Yoruba girl. My father wasn't as vocal as my mother. He'd often remain quiet about the matter. However, there was one time he alluded to it. It was the very first time that I left for New York City. He drove me to the airport and said, "Find someone that makes you happy."

Processing that statement now, I wonder if he knew that I was gay. The only time I remember not living a guarded life was in New Orleans. I would smile freely, laugh without fear, and say "I love you" out loud without restraint. That changed in Iowa when I lost the bliss that ignorance brings and became aware. Still, my father had to know because he'd seen all my transitions. If he knew, he chose to remain silent, accepting my self-imposed repression for the better good of the community and our family.

After we ate dinner, similarly to how I broke the news that I was changing my major in college, I came out to my parents. My mother spoke first. "What did we do to deserve this? How could this happen? Are you sure you're gay? You've never had a girlfriend; how can you be sure you're gay? Does this mean you won't have children?" The questions kept pouring in. I did my best to answer them, to put her at ease, one by one, but I could tell she wasn't absorbing my responses, only trying to catch me at a moment of weakness. My father remained quiet. After my mother exhausted herself, she looked towards my father for support. He was seated beside her on the couch adjacent to me. While my mother was on edge, hoping to use the force of her will to change my mind, my father was sitting with his back fully supported, his eyes slowly shifting between my mom and me. Her eyes eventually met his, and then he looked at me and said, "Are you happy?" To which I replied, "Yes." Then he said, "Then it is okay with me." My mother looked at him, surprised, but didn't follow up with a comment. We sat silently until my brother and sister entered the room and turned on the television.

I was shocked at how easy it was to come out to my father. Like my mother, I figured there would be many questions, pushback, and clear signs of disappointment. Growing up, I saw my parents desperately try to fit in and live according to strict moral codes of conduct, which guaranteed their safety against discrimination. On top of that, I saw them struggle with the tricky dance of living up to the expectations of other Nigerian families. I think my father was tired, and I believe he didn't want that life for his children—he just wanted us to be ourselves and happy, something I think he was denied.

My world opened up more after coming out. With my family, I was able to share another dimension of myself. My mother continued to call weekly to ask how I was doing with the added curiosity about the men I dated. She applied the same rubric test for women to men based on their personalities, career, religion, and family life. "Now, tell me about their family. What do their parents do? Are they Christians? What race are they? Send me a picture—are they on social media?" It was a new source of stress for me but welcomed. For the first time in my life, I had nothing to hide. I felt this same freedom with my siblings, too, especially my younger brother, who took the news of me coming out so well. He, like my father, just wanted to know if I was happy. Fast forward a year later, my brother visited and grabbed dinner with a guy I'd been dating for two months named Jacob.

I met Jacob through my first job in New York. He worked in the business development arm of the nonprofit, searching for and responding to grant opportunities. His work ethic struck me. He'd often stay late, past 10:00 p.m. some nights, piecing together data and staff bios to apply for grants that our executive director found last minute in hopes of securing funding and keeping our shoestring organization afloat.

Besides his work ethic, I was immediately drawn to his looks. He had a rich olive skin tone and deep brown hair—almost black, thick with waves that moved as he walked. I couldn't determine his ethnicity, but I later learned he was Jewish, with roots tracing back to Romania. He had a sturdy build and was the same height as me—but more athletic. He had a sharp sense of style, always wearing a pressed button-down shirt with slim-fit pants and colored sneakers with white soles.

Jacob interacted the most with staff in other divisions to retrieve data for grants—he'd hold agency-wide meetings, making them fun—starting them off by telling jokes or quoting lyrics from his favorite nineties hip hop songs. I watched him effortlessly navigate various stakeholder meetings with policymakers, donors, and the businesses we served—always finding a connection to build a foundation of mutual trust.

Our worlds intersected when it was time to reapply for the grant that funded the program I managed. Jacob scheduled a one-on-one meeting with me to review the goals set by the funder and the outcome of our work to date. He also wanted me to recommend success stories of businesses we'd help highlight in his report. I prepared for the meeting feverishly—understanding that Jacob was highly proficient at his job, I wanted to make an excellent first impression. I even tried to dress up that day, wearing a gray button-down with khaki pants, an olive-green blazer, and white dress sneakers.

"Eddie, how are you? Looking sharp, man. I don't think I've ever seen you wear a blazer...is this all for me?"

I was embarrassed and stuttered out my response. I eventually got the words out. "Oh yeah, I went shopping recently and decided to wear a few of the items today."

Jacob smiled and said, "Well, you look great! Reviewing our contract with the funder, I peeked at your internal files to pull outcome numbers. I'd like this to be more of an informal conversation about your experience with service delivery and firms we can highlight in the report. Are you interested in meeting at the coffee shop next door?"

I agreed, and we went to the local coffee shop around the block. For the first hour, we discussed work-related topics, and into the second, we transitioned into our personal lives.

"Eddie, you have an interesting last name. Where does it come from?"

It was a question I was used to. "It's a Yoruba last name. My parents immigrated from Nigeria and came from Lagos State."

Jacob nodded. "I thought you were from Nigeria. My roommate in college was Nigerian. I remember going to his family home and tasting Nigerian food for the first time. I fell in love with fufu with chicken pepper soup! You know, there's a fantastic Nigerian restaurant in Bed-Stuy. If you're interested, we should go."

The flirtation from Jacob felt foreign to me. I'd conditioned myself to chase others, not to be chased. At the time, I believed it was my burden of proof to justify value. To be the person wooed felt wrong, against the natural order of things; I couldn't accept it.

"Oh, yeah, that would be great," I said, believing the request wasn't serious; however, he immediately proved me wrong.

"So, are you free next Thursday, or how about the following Thursday? Let's put something on the books!"

Weeks later, we ended up going to that restaurant. I learned more about his family and his journey as a gay man. Jacob was born in Brooklyn but grew up in Jersey. His family was a similar size to mine—three children, although he was the middle child with an older brother and younger sister. Jacob came out as gay in middle school and was met with little resistance from his parents; it was celebrated during his bar mitzvah. He had his first boyfriend during his sophomore year of high school, who he broke up with shortly after his first year in college. From then on, Jacob had ample practice with dating men and being in relationships. I was envious as I listened to him recount the trials and tribulations of dating in New York. Unlike him, who was confident and reassured—traits reinforced by family, friends, and his life experiences—I was not. Despite coming out to my parents, an uneasiness lurked overhead in embracing my sexuality. Something in me had difficulty letting go of the need to hide—blend in, accept less, but give more. Frankly, I was surprised that he was interested in me. Unlike me, Jacob was an experienced weightlifter in confidently accepting and loving his body and mind—that feeling was foreign to me, a heavier load I had yet to learn how to carry.

***

Snapping out of pondering my past, I arrive at the psychic's office three minutes before my scheduled appointment. The storefront is visible from the street with a neon sign that reads *Psychic Readings.* I walk into the building, which is organized with small boutique shops. The soothsayer's office is situated to the right at the entrance. At the door, I see a sign: *Be right back.* So, I lean against the wall and wait, drifting back into my memories, this time thinking of Jacob and that first date.

***

Thursday night came. Hours before our meeting I searched my closet. Jacob was always so well put together. I wanted to impress him but was overthinking everything. Should I wear jeans and a T-shirt or be more formal with a button-down shirt and khakis? I chose a combination of the two, with a white oxford shirt, dark blue denim, boots, and a jacket to account for the mid-fall weather.

We decided to meet up at the restaurant at 7:00 p.m. I got there on the dot and found him inside sitting in the center of the restaurant. He wore a tastefully plaid maroon and navy shirt with khaki pants, black dress shoes, and a brown sports coat with cream speckles.

"Eddie, it's good to see you. You look amazing! Come sit down," he said after standing up and giving me a hug. "Have you ever been here before?"

"No, to be honest. I've never gone to a Nigerian restaurant; I didn't even realize that they exist," I said with embarrassment to this Jewish man who likely knew more about Nigeria than I did.

"No worries at all, I got you covered. I've tried everything on the menu and will happily order for the two of us. Let's start with drinks. If you've never tried it you have to taste the palm wine–inspired cocktail. I've been told you can only try palm wine in Nigeria, but this drink mimics the smooth, milky, sweet-and-sour taste of the real thing."

For the rest of the meal, Jacob took the lead ordering food, inquiring about my thoughts on the flavors, whether or not it was something my mom would cook. He was inventive, hanging on to my every word and following up with thoughtful questions. He seemed genuinely interested in me, which I found baffling. I wasn't used to talking so much about myself, and I started to feel self-conscious. Jacob recognized the change in my disposition and said, "I'm sorry if I'm asking a lot of questions. I just want to learn more about you. I've noticed you for a long time. You don't say much, but the times that you do speak I always want more. I'm seizing my opportunity."

After that night, Jacob and I started to see each other more often and eventually started to date. We moved in together a year and a half later. I gave up my apartment in Crown Heights and moved to Prospect Heights, Brooklyn. It's funny how it all started with him asking me for coffee, and then dinner. Now, waiting for my appointment to start with the psychic, I understand. Jacob built a foundation early in our relationship. Bricks are marked by adjectives associated with curiosity, interest, and affirmation. Jacob was a fully realized person who cared about himself and the people he chose to bring into his life. I trusted him, but I didn't trust myself. This unresolved issue would be the crack that would break the life we sought to build together.

5

Drinks

Pheeew, I breathe out as I exit my apartment building. Thank God it's Saturday. I have no appointments or obligations; I'm free to do with my time as I wish. The cold air hits my skin, prompting a tingling sensation as the blood rushes to the surface to compensate for the sudden change in the surrounding temperature. I greet another resident as I exit, and they enter the building. After a few stretches, I start my run. It doesn't take long for my mind to return to the past.

***

I'm perpetually late, and it's an issue that's gotten me in a lot of trouble. It's not that I don't value other people's time or that I'm trying to be disrespectful—I've just genuinely forgotten or been overly optimistic with my time management. I had every intention of meeting with Eddie for coffee, but at the last minute I got dragged into a meeting with one of my vendors and forgot to text him that I wasn't free. He messaged me, but I kept my phone silent and saw his note two hours later. I intended to reply immediately after work, but I was running late for a date. Anyway, he beat me to it. And wrote:

Alan, didn't we plan to meet for coffee today at 3 pm? I waited for 30 minutes. I sent you a message to see if you were running late and didn't hear from you; you have yet to respond or even apologize for not showing up. This behavior has happened several times, with you arriving late—with no apology. It's hurtful. I took time out of my schedule to meet you for an event you've scheduled and got stood up. I feel like you don't respect my time.

Damn, I fucked up. I was shocked to see this text from Eddie. I've never had a friend be so direct about his disappointment. I froze when I read it. Eddie wasn't someone who got upset easily. He was right; I was late meeting with him several times prior. However, Eddie would say it was okay each time, gently asking me to be more considerate. Besides, I was doing better, going against the grain of my typical behavior. In my perspective, punctuality was only essential at work. However, Eddie once said something that struck me: "Showing up on time is a sign of thoughtfulness and intention. I am purposefully setting aside time to spend with you, not because I have to but because I want to. I hope you feel the same way about me." I did; I truly enjoyed our time together. I never felt judged by him. Each time we met, I felt better. There was a lot of shit happening in my life, and he was an oasis to retreat to. Wanting to make it right immediately, I wrote:

Eddie, I'm sorry. It was a hectic day. I had every intention of coming but was pulled into a last-minute meeting. I'm also sorry that this has been a pattern. I didn't know. How can I make this up to you? Can we meet up tomorrow to discuss this more? I'm sorry.

Minutes later, after sending my text message, I looked to see if Eddie had read it. He had but hadn't responded, which was not like him. Eddie usually replied to my texts minutes after I'd sent them. I was worried. Had I offended my only friend at work? Eddie was someone I could genuinely open up to, and I valued the advice I got from him. The truth was that he was becoming more than just a colleague—he provided emotional support that I wasn't used to receiving, especially from other men.

When we first started grabbing coffee, in addition to all the shit that was going on with work, I was in a very unsatisfying relationship. I'd met Ashley at a house party in Bushwick. She was originally from Hawaii—a self-proclaimed surfer girl who was twenty-four, Asian, thin, and worked in graphic design— one hundred percent my type, at least on paper.

There was a lot that I liked about Ashley. She let me do what I wanted to her sexually. I'd videotape our encounters—she was very submissive. However, that contributed to the problem I had with her—she didn't have a mind of her own; when we were together, I did all the talking, and she just listened. The only original thoughts that would sprout from her were about Harry Styles or some dumbass fantasy show that, for the love of god, I can't recall the name of.

Ashley was sweet, but I wasn't looking to recreate my high school relationship. Inadvertently, I found myself trying to sabotage it. For instance, I'd purposely wait a day or two to respond to her text messages, ignore topics she brought up, or respond with emojis. I'd overbook my nights, often showing up late to my commitments with her. I remember one time I'd invited her to my apartment. I passed out on the couch. None of my roommates were home. I didn't hear it when she arrived and rang the doorbell several times. She sent text messages that I didn't notice either. With no response from me, she left. I got up later that evening, remembering that we had planned to meet, and realized that she had come over but that I'd missed her. I figured I'd apologize to her the next day and went back to sleep. Well, the next day came, I apologized, and she accepted it. Retrospectively, I realized that it was bad behavior. I was abusive, acting out what I learned earlier in life. I guess I rationalized my actions through the desire for someone to challenge me, which Ashley wasn't equipped to do. No surprise, we broke up. Or, instead, I broke up with her after attempting to do it three times previously. After that breakup, it felt like an avalanche of bad things happened to me.

After a year of living together, my roommates asked me to leave. It was explained to me that all the small things added up, and in their words, I was "inconsiderate" and "didn't contribute equally to household expenses." To be honest, I was okay to leave. They were douchebags—always flaunting their money, contributing no real benefit to society. Besides, my brother Noah had recently moved to the city, and I was happy to room with him.

Noah had landed a job as an engineer at a large construction firm based in Manhattan. He had been fired from his old job back home in Pennsylvania. The reason: he cursed his boss for criticizing his final project report and refusing to take any feedback. While discussing it over the phone, we laughed. As a family, we took pride in being stubborn smart-asses who held their ground with less-than-smart people. In talking, we'd quickly recognized that we both needed a fresh start. I suggested he look for opportunities in New York, where he found something quickly.

Noah and I had our issues in the past with his anger manage-ment problems, but I'd hoped our relationship would change now as grown men. I needed family around me, someone that got me, who I didn't have to apologize to for being myself. Our relationship was far from perfect; we fought all the time growing up—but again, I hoped that as men in our late twenties and early thirties who had been experiencing tough times, we'd figure out how to be there for each other. Well, I was very wrong. We constantly fought about everything—from buying food for the house and paying rent on time to over-drinking and bringing up old shit from childhood. My brother hated that he got the brunt of abuse from our mother and blamed me and my brother for allowing him to take the fall for everything and never sticking up for him. The truth was that Noah was a jerk who never took responsibility for anything and expected things to be given to him. I resented that he tried to control me or act as if he knew better because he was older. When we went out together, Noah brought up embarrassing shit like me wetting the bed or flashing my dick at a public pool when I was fucking five years old. He purposely tried to make me look like an idiot in front of my friends or like the dopey brother that couldn't wipe his ass unless he was around to give me toilet paper.

It all came to a head one night after heavy drinking. We'd been arguing about household supplies and groceries earlier that morning. Noah felt that I didn't contribute and wanted me to pay more that month for rent to cover the difference. His calculation was way off. He wanted me to spend $250 more on rent. Yes, he contributed more to household shit, but I can't believe it was that much more. I refused. We dropped the argument and went to work that day but came to blows that evening.

"You're a fucking prick," said Noah. "I'm constantly paying for shit. You never contribute, not even a fucking thank you. You've always been like this, never once showing fucking gratitude. Alan, you either pay the difference in rent or pay me what I'm owed." His voice was firm as he stared ahead, standing near the kitchen sink with a glass of water.

"What the fuck? I never told you to get anything for the house. You decided that on your own. I'm not paying for shit I barely use," I said by the cabinet, reaching for a bag of chips with a beer on the counter next to me.

"Alan, oh my god, are you fucking kidding me? Who the hell do you think bought the chips you're eating and the beer you're drinking? You're a fucking leech, a fucking parasite. You take and never give. You've always been like this—even as kids, you always thought only about yourself," Noah said with increasing agitation, his voice rising in volume.

"Oh, here we go again, bringing up old shit from the past. You're a fucking baby—you can't get over shit. Is this about how Mom fucking beat your ass? Man, you deserved every bit of it. You were always getting into dumb shit, and you were dumb as fuck. You constantly made us look bad as a family; I'm surprised you're even working now. You were a fuckup— actually, you still are now."

Shortly after uttering those words, cold water met my face along with the hardness of the glass, which sharply cut my cheek. Before I could realize it, Noah grabbed me and punched me square in the face—now injuring my nose. I got my bearings and landed a punch on his shoulders, but my brother was much stronger than me, partly due to his training for a triathlon. He kept pounding on me, his rage bringing me back to when we fought as kids. His anger seemed to have no end, and I couldn't contain it. The floodgates were open. He grabbed me by the shirt, dragged me to the door, and kicked me out. He wouldn't let me back into the apartment. I had to call a friend to let me stay with him for the night. We never made up. I had to get my stuff out of the apartment while he was away at work, and

I ended up staying with a friend for close to a month before I landed at another place in Williamsburg. As for my brother, he finished his lease and left immediately afterward for Austin, Texas. Our relationship has never been the same since.

So, the text message from Eddie scared me. I couldn't lose a friend now. I needed Eddie in my life. He gave me stability. I trusted him. I opened up to him about everything happening in my life, and he listened to me; Eddie cared. We met up the next day, and out of nowhere, I just cried.

***

I eventually agreed to meet Alan for coffee the next day. We met in the Seaport neighborhood in the vicinity of Pier 17. I was three minutes late and found him waiting patiently on a bench. He greeted me with a smile. We hugged, and then I began the conversation by asking him how the day was going—and then afterward, I immediately started to discuss being stood up the day before and other patterns I saw in our friendship that I didn't like. I could see tears welling up in Alan's eyes. I stopped and asked him if he was okay. I'd never seen him express such sadness before, and it caught me off guard.

"I'm sorry," Alan said, "I didn't mean to disrespect you. You are important to me. Sometimes, I get lost in my work and forget the time. It's no excuse, but I'm sorry. I can't have you being mad at me. Our friendship means a lot to me."

"Alan, it's okay. Our friendship isn't ending; I just want you to be considerate of my time." It was a line I'd used before, but I said it reassuringly. "I care about you and our friendship too, but there are too many moments where you do all the talking, and I'm expected to listen. Well, I need you to listen to me too. I need you to show up for me; in small ways, like being on time or responsive to text messages. A little can go a long way. It shows that you care but also that you respect me and my time. I just want to feel reciprocity from you. Alan, you completely disregarded me yesterday, and not even sending me a text that you couldn't make coffee highlighted that imbalance in our friendship. It hurt my feelings."

I can't believe those words came out of my mouth. I'd never so honestly shared my discontentment with friends. I generally took bad behavior directed my way, but I knew I wanted more from Alan, so I took a chance and revealed something real.

"Can I make it up to you? Maybe I can treat you to drinks and possibly dinner after work?" Alan said beside me, his shoulders touching mine.

After a pause, I looked at Alan directly and said, "Sure, that would be nice."

6

Hanging Out

Alan made good on his promise. The next day, he took me to a bar in the east village. We left immediately after work. He came to my desk with a big smile and asked, "Are you ready?" I replied, "Yep, just sending my last email." I hurriedly typed a few lines before clicking the send button.

On the train to the bar, Alan recounted his day. The train rocked back and forth as we held on to the support bar. In the corner of my eye, I spotted an open pizza box with two half-eaten pizza slices. One slice lay plainly on the floor near us, filling the crowded train with its aroma. I barely noticed the smell, though. I was fixated on the words coming out of Alan's mouth, even though I can't remember what he said. However, I do recall the stream of sweat running down his face. I noticed his white shirt, wet around his chest, and the sleeves haphazardly rolled up his arms. I admired how his gray dress pants fit around his thighs, and when we got off the train and I was walking behind him, his ass. Alan would often wear tight-fitting pants. Sometimes, the pants were obscenely tight. I initially questioned his sexuality. On Fridays, he would wear these black chinos that clearly showed the shape of his ass and the silhouette of his penis—every time he wore them, I would compliment him, encouraging him to wear them more often.

I further let my mind wander as we exited the train and headed to the bar. What would sex be like with Alan? He was probably a top. A take-control kind of guy. Likely not attentive, wanting to be pleased as opposed to pleasing. Alan was cocky. Overwhelmingly confident in himself and his abilities to charm others. This understanding was based on the conversations I'd had with him about dating in New York and his lack of issues in finding dates. He was arrogant, but still, I was curious.

When we arrived at the bar, he ordered us both drinks. Alan asked what sour beers they had, and I asked to see their cocktail menu. After we received our drinks and settled in, conversation flowed with every sip and gulp.

"Alan, thanks for organizing this. I love this bar." Sun flooded the space from above, giving life to the many plants filling every crevice. The white subway tile from floor to ceiling enhanced the luminance of the interior. The gold of the bar rails and stools, capped in black leather, provided regal charm, and the carefully placed flower bouquet made the event feel even more special.

"No problem, Eddie. It's the least I can do. I'm sorry about yesterday. Tonight's on me. So...you're a cocktail guy?"

"Yeah, I've never liked beer. I don't see the appeal, but a good cocktail—well, you can't beat it."

"That's a shame, 'cause man, I fucking love beer. Especially sour IPAs. I've always liked the combination of tart, fruity, and acidic flavors; it's like sweet nectar from the gods," Alan said right before he finished his third chug.

For an hour, we discussed work—but after getting my second drink and Alan ordering his third, the conversation started to get more personal.

"Alan, tell me about your family. Do you have brothers? Sisters? I know you grew up in Pennsylvania, but outside of that, I know relatively little about your family," I said, wanting to move away from work-related topics and get to know him more.

"Sure. I have two brothers. Ryan's the oldest and Noah is the middle child. I'm the youngest in the group. My mom's a teacher, and my dad is a traveling doctor. We grew up in a small town outside of Scranton in Pennsylvania." Alan paused momentarily, grabbed his beer, and swallowed another mouthful. Afterward, he slowly set it down, looked at me, and said, "To be honest, I'm not particularly close with my family. My brother just kicked me out of the apartment we shared. We got into a blowout fight over petty shit. Ryan has mental health issues and has been increasingly isolating himself over the years, and I truly hate my mom. She never had anything positive to say to me, and growing up she made me feel small as shit, and my dad, well, I barely speak to him. The times we've connected, I do have good memories. He and I traveled to Peru the summer before my junior year in high school. He was doing aid work there, and I spent my entire summer with him, which was great considering he was away most summers. I'd gotten in trouble the year prior for going to this house party and drinking. That trip was meant for us to bond, but afterward, it felt like he didn't try anymore. Our conversations over the phone are usually surface too, and we talk about taking another trip together but he always has an excuse not to follow through." Alan paused, again taking another drink, and looked to me for a response.

"I don't think any family is perfect; we all have issues. I felt my parents cared more about what other people thought of them

52

than what they thought about themselves or us as their kids. But they did their best to raise us, and they're trying to do better in knowing us now. It's strange, though, because I've had to readjust my image of them and of myself." I was surprised to hear the words come out as they did; I've never given myself space to process my childhood—always reluctant to utter words that painted my parents in a less favorable light. However, the words held meaning, and it felt like a relief to acknowledge them.

"Besides your family, tell me about your friends. Do you have people you're close to here or at home?" I said, attempting to move the conversation to a lighter topic.

"Yeah, I do have friends," Alan said, noticeably more upbeat. "My good friend Cody is visiting me in the fall. We've been friends since junior high. We fell out briefly while I was in college, but we recently reconnected."

"That's awesome! Tell me about him," I said, eagerly hoping to get more of a glimpse of the type of people he surrounded himself with. Alan proceeded to talk about Cody and all his endearing aspects. "Cody, his ability to befriend anyone. Growing up, I loved going over to his house. I thought he had the ideal family—and his parents were open-minded. There were no off-limits topics: drug use, sex, politics. It was a household where ideas were shared freely, unlike mine.

We were both on the swim team, so I spent a lot of time with his parents. My parents never supported me in anything that wasn't related to academics. But his parents actively supported him in everything he did. I admired that; I swear I was at his house so often that I became an honorary member of their family. That's why it sucked when we lost touch," Alan said, staring at his drink. "College life just got hectic for me. I was dating a ton. I just lost track of our friendship." The noise in the bar seemed to quiet as he looked up from his drink, and his eyes met mine. "Anyway, I'm glad we have reconnected. Since being in New York, I've reminisced about growing up in Pennsylvania, belonging to something—a community."

***

I enter Prospect Park at the entrance near Grand Army Plaza. I'm prepared to run two loops around the perimeter, roughly six and a half miles. There's a sea of tents for the weekly farmers market. I make my way through strollers, dogs, and cyclists and then realize that I've forgotten my headphones, so I use my surroundings for stimuli and motivation, but ten minutes into the run, memories of Eddie catch up to me.

***

I was happy to smooth things over with Eddie. He seemed to enjoy drinks, and we genuinely had a great time. I surprised myself with the level of ease I experienced with him. People aren't generally that interested in learning about things like your childhood friend or your relationship with your family, let alone each member, but he was. Eddie seemed to care and listened to me so intently, his eyes fixed on me. It was flattering. He didn't say much; however, I did appreciate him sharing about his family and assuring me that mine was entirely fucked up.

From then on, we continued to meet at least once a week. I'd always make it a point to message Eddie well before our scheduled coffee to make sure that he was free or to change the date if I wasn't available. Often, instead of coffee, I proposed that we grab drinks instead. Or, at times, I'd convince him to meet closer to 4:30 p.m. and grab early drinks.

As my friendship developed with Eddie, my relationship with Ashley deteriorated. I'd broken up with her three times. The first time was genuine; I realized we weren't compatible intellectually, but seeing her pain exposed made me renege. I attempted to view our relationship through her eyes, as Eddie suggested on one occasion, but the relationship didn't feel right. I looked for issues to initiate breakups the other two times. For instance, the second time, I told her I was breaking up with her due to her lack of curiosity about me or my family life; the third and last time, it boiled down to her lack of career and personal aspirations. To be fair, Ashley had no genuine ambitions outside of being my girlfriend. It may appear that I'm being narcissistic or hypercritical—I realize I have my issues too, but she never told me what they were. In her eyes, I was perfect. I needed more. I wanted her to need more too. Plus, I found myself comparing my interactions with her to Eddie. After all, he became my confidant, intimately aware of my relationship challenges and the back-and-forth between Ashley and myself. Eddie tried to help me see her side but never made me feel wrong about how I felt. In the fall, Ashley and I split, but I was okay with it, partly because it meant I could spend more time with Eddie.

Our friendship transitioned into the weekends. I remember the first time I reached out. I was supposed to take this girl on a date to see my favorite DJ. The day of the concert, she flaked. I immediately called Eddie, and he was down. I'm sure it wasn't his taste in music, but Eddie was always available to try new things, which was a defining characteristic I appreciated. He knew none of the songs but danced his heart out, sweating with the crowd and me throughout the concert. Afterward, we went to my favorite bar in Greenpoint and left at 3:00 am. He made himself available to hang out—running through Prospect

Park, attending comedy shows, going to bars, even attending niche policy lectures. Eddie met me at all levels of intellectual curiosity.

I'm not naive; I had a feeling that he liked me. I've seen these patterns before with women trying to gain approval by doing stuff to please me. But, with Eddie, it felt different. There was enjoyment there. It didn't feel like an act, but he participated actively. Also, there wasn't the pressure of sexual attraction, at least initially. I don't think he expected anything from me on that front. He seemed to simply enjoy spending time with me.

I will own up to my part in setting things in the wrong direction between Eddie and me. A coworker was having a going away party. I waited for Eddie to finish up at work, and we went together to join the celebration. An hour or two into it, I started drinking. Eddie laughed at one of my jokes as we stood far from the crowd. I finished my drink and asked to taste his, which he offered. As I grabbed it from him, I kissed him on his neck. I don't know why I did it. But I remember the look of surprise on his face. I was surprised. Maybe I did it because I thought he wanted me to. He didn't say anything. He didn't acknowledge it. I suggested that we leave and go dancing, his choice of place. So, we settled up with our checks and headed into Williamsburg to this place called Metropolitan—a gay bar. We got more drinks and started dancing together. I kissed him two more times on the neck there. During the second time, before he could react, two guys started hitting on us.

***

This all started when Alan kissed me. *Why did he have to lead me on?* I think, looking at my phone to see the time. It's ten minutes past my appointment with the psychic. *Maybe I should*

56

just leave. This was a bad idea. I start to go and see a woman walking toward the door.

"I'm sorry I'm late. I had an emergency that I had to attend to. I need to quickly set up the space. Can you wait a few more minutes?" she says, appearing genuinely apologetic.

"Sure, not a problem," I say. She enters the room and starts setting up while I remain outside, wrapped in thought.

***

"Hey, how's it going?" one of them said to Alan with a drunken smile.

"We're good," Alan said, with a pleased look that he was getting attention so early.

The other guy directly stood next to me, clearly not as drunk as his friend but equally bold—patting me on the back, greeting me with his name, and asking for mine. "Hey, man, I'm Greg. What's your name?"

"Hey, Greg, I'm Eddie."

As soon as I said my name, he quickly asked in a loud voice for me, Alan, and his friend to hear, "So Eddie, are you two together?"

I looked at Alan and saw the big smile on his face, egging me on to say yes. I didn't oblige. I said no.

I received a text message from Jacob during my coworker's going away party. He wanted to know when I was planning to come home. He'd made a vegetarian lasagna and offered to heat it up when I returned. Initially, I responded that I'd be back in an hour, but after the kiss, I wrote back and said I'd be home much later because we were going to another place and he shouldn't worry about me. It was a knee-jerk reaction. I pushed all guilt aside. I wanted more time with Alan. It wasn't until

57

the Metropolitan that the illusion broke: I was not single; I had someone who loved me and cared enough to make sure I had warm food waiting for me. Why was I here? What was I doing? *I'm not single; this feels wrong.*

The pair lit up with confidence and asked us if we wanted a drink; Alan said no, that we were about to leave, but thanked them. As they walked away, Alan looked at me, started to laugh, and continued to dance, seemingly pleased with himself and how he handled the interaction. We left shortly afterward.

By that point, Alan was drunk. I lost count of the number of drinks he'd consumed. On the other hand, I'd likely had three—well, really, two and a half. Alan drank half of my first drink during the going away party. With his hand wrapped around my neck, I supported Alan as we walked outside the bar. I insisted that he catch a cab, but after a block of walking, we reached the subway, which he was determined to take. We headed into the subway, walked down the stairs, and arrived at the turnstiles. I watched him pull out his metro card and start to swipe when he paused, looked back at me, and said, "I love you, man." He kissed me again on the cheek, swiped his card, and walked unsteadily to his train.

7

I'm not gay

"The room is ready; please come in," says the psychic with a closed-mouth smile. Her words break my concentration.

"Oh, okay...thank you." I hadn't gotten a chance to closely look at her until now. She is much younger than I expected, likely in her early thirties, with honeysuckle blonde hair and fair skin. She introduces herself as Elena, and by the sound of her accent, I gather she's from an Eastern European country. I enter the room and notice a row of candles lit on a small console table and sticks of burning incense that fill the room with an aroma laced with sandalwood. The walls in the room are painted lavender with framed references to the zodiac signs and other mystical iconography unknown to me. Elena prominently displays her prices; I plan to do a psychic reading, which costs one hundred dollars.

Elena directs me to sit on a chair next to a small round table covered with a white blanket with white round tassels at its edges. On the table are tarot cards neatly stacked. We spoke on the phone before our meeting to discuss the services, so there is no need for an additional explanation in person. When we're both seated, she stretches her hands over the table and asks for mine. "Clear your mind and focus on what you want to uncover."

I try to do as she asked, but my mind focuses on my past.

***

Immediately after leaving Alan, it felt like I jumped back on solid ground. Before that moment, the world was spinning. Everything was happening so fast—like I was on an invisible merry-go-round, spinning out of control by the hand of some unruly child until I had to abruptly jump off. Once on the ground, dizzy from the kisses, I felt motion sickness and was confused by Alan's declaration of love.

Our departure gave me a moment to breathe and process everything that happened. If I'm honest with myself, I've wanted Alan from the moment I saw him. His actions permitted me to admit my desire. I was attracted to him, but I also cared about him; well, maybe I just liked how he made me feel and how I felt about myself around him. Was I even sure what I felt? My thoughts felt jumbled, still mixed up from all the spinning. One thing I was sure about was that hours with Alan made me feel good.

After all, Alan sought me out for advice and continued to pursue a friendship with me. I liked how our relationship had evolved into something more personable and intimate, flowering into kisses along my neck. It may be uneventful to some, but for me, those kisses proved that Alan wanted me. The kisses affirmed that a markedly handsome man desired me and that I was desirable. I felt the warmth of desire, the sensation evident by the tingling that still lingered along my neck. I replayed our exchanges a hundred times as I rode in a cab from Williamsburg back to Prospect Heights and Jacob.

Life with Jacob was stable. We'd moved into a beautiful apartment in Prospect Heights. We both had left the nonprofit world, where we'd met, and continued our climbs along our respective career ladders, leading me to the economic development corporation and Jacob to a philanthropic foundation based in New York with satellite offices scattered internationally. The foundation funded infrastructure projects in developing countries to spur economic development by helping isolated communities access transportation networks. Jacob was hired to help the organization review project proposals and select new grantees. Due to the nature of this work, Jacob traveled for weeks to check onsite potential infrastructure projects, listen to organizations' pitches, and join the funders to award grants or visit the completed projects. His primary objective was to ensure that the foundation chose partners with compelling stories and projects who could accomplish the work and impact the community the most. When he was in town, he spent many hours poring over new and existing projects and preparing for his next trip.

Despite his travels and the intensity that his work required, Jacob did his best to make me feel comfortable. He showed love through action. His love language shone through his intentionality. Before each trip, Jacob took inventory of the food in our apartment. The day before he left on a long journey, like clockwork, he'd visit the local grocery store to restock the refrigerator and cabinets with all my favorite foods and snacks, making sure that I had at least one meal I could make for a week. Jacob would clean the house from top to bottom, removing the dust bunnies lurking behind the furniture in obscure crevices. He even trekked to the laundromat several blocks away to do laundry, leaving behind the fresh scent of dryer sheets throughout our home.

However, the action I appreciated the most was the card and occasional flowers he'd leave behind. In the card, he always wrote a lyric from a song that reminded me of his love for me. But my love language paled in comparison to his. I worked to create a beautiful home for us. I'd infused our apartment with greenery and colorful art. I bravely entered his world, dotted with well-rounded people versed in all corners of discourse, doing my best to show that I was worthy of his gifts. However, Jacob was always affirming, constantly communicating the status I held in his heart. We had a healthy love life. He helped me feel free, explore pleasure, and truly discover what felt good. Initially, I preferred to make love in the dark, but every time I turned the light off, Jacob would switch it back on, saying, "I want to see you." Eventually, I embraced the light.

I loved Jacob. I was intellectually and sexually attracted to him. And I felt safe with him, but still—I was unfulfilled. I was curious about other men. I'd only started dating men not even a full year before I met Jacob. I can admit that as much as I cared for Jacob, I was dealing with my internal issues of not feeling enough, particularly regarding my desirability. I needed validation from someone else to prove I was truly worthy of love. That someone else could want me as he did. When I met Alan, that restlessness grew roots and sprouted above the surface. The green became evident to me, and instead of pulling it out of me, I watered it and allowed it to grow.

I had opportunities to confront my restlessness with Jacob. During Yom Kippur, the Jewish holiday of atonement, Jacob directly asked me if I was happy, if I felt loved by him. It had been a week since my encounter with Alan, and I believe Jacob sensed my distance. It was his superpower, ever observant and keyed into my emotional state. I was distracted. I hadn't seen or heard from Alan since our encounter. I was anxious. Did Alan regret his actions? Was he keeping his distance from me? I didn't know. Jacob and I were en route to visit with his family, so without batting an eye, I said, "Yes, I'm happy. I love you." I missed my chance to have an honest conversation, to engage in transparency, to atone for the guilt that quickly morphed into the shame of the realization that I wanted more but didn't know exactly what.

***

I'm halfway through my run. I completed one lap around the park and am now back at the entrance near Grand Army Plaza. I hate running in this section because your stride is always compromised by the pedestrians entering the path, forcing you to weave through a web of people unaware of the obstacles they're creating. However, once clear, I regain focus, revving up like an engine, accelerating and increasing speed until I'm at a pace that allows me to coast and fall back into my thoughts.

***

Eddie and I were scheduled to meet up for coffee on Wednesday. I hadn't communicated with him since the night we hung out two Fridays ago. Honestly, I knew what I was doing when I kissed him. I also knew that he wanted it and was attracted to me. I liked the attention and wanted to show it, but I wasn't sexually attracted to Eddie. My feelings were complicated. I meant what I said—I loved him. He was a great listener and became a better friend. I'd never had the type of relationship with another man as I had with Eddie. I wanted to show appreciation, but I admit it wasn't the best approach.

"Hey, Eddie, how's it going, man?" I greeted Eddie like usual, as if it were any other day—just as we'd done when meeting for coffee many times over the past year. I hoped we'd ignore what happened and mutually agree, without words, to move on.

"I'm good. It's good to see you, and I'm happy we kept our coffee meeting today. I missed you last week. I hope you're well?" Eddie said with a bright smile. I was drawn to Eddie's smile; seeing it always made me feel good. I appreciated that Eddie poured positivity into our encounters, especially during the first moments of seeing each other; he made you feel like you were the only person in the room. Eddie was a hugger. Whenever we met, he gave me full-body hugs lasting a few additional seconds longer than a regular embrace, long enough to notice. No pats on the back included like with the customary hugs between my other guy friends, which always felt performative. It was when we hugged that I noticed his smell. Eddie smelled like a faint combination of pancakes and maple syrup. I asked him if he used a particular lotion or cologne, and he told me he used a scented pomade called burnt sugar. I grew to love it, breathing it in with each hug. To this day, when I have pancakes, I think of Eddie.

I offered to get Eddie a coffee. He generally got an iced coffee with oat milk and opted for coconut milk as a substitute. Eddie had a sweet tooth. He'd often get a pastry to share, leaving me with the lion's share of the treat. I was neither here nor there when it came to sweets, but I liked that Eddie thought to share them with me. I asked him if he wanted something else other than coffee. The place we went to was known for its donuts, and I knew he had a weakness for the glazed kind. His eyes lit up with the thought and rested on me as he said, "No, thank you."

I went to the counter to order and bring back our coffees while he searched for a table for us to sit at.

We started with small talk about the weather, then shifted to work, politics, and gossip in the office. I could tell when Eddie was preoccupied, though. It seemed like something was on the tip of his tongue, like he was ready to yell it out but held back, scared of the answer he might hear.

"Alan, can we talk about what happened the last time we hung out?"

"Sure, I've been meaning to bring it up. Look, I'm sorry, man. I had a lot to drink that night. I've been told that I get touchy-feely when I'm drunk. It's something I've dealt with since college. I remember girls telling me I'm overly flirty, although I've never received any complaints. But hopefully you didn't get the wrong idea," I said confidently, leg folded, with my left ankle set on my right knee. I took a sip of my coffee as I watched Eddie change position in his chair, grab his coffee, and sip through his straw.

"It's okay; I didn't mind. I actually liked it. The whole night was great. I had fun. It's also okay if you like me that way," he said reassuringly, with his eyes focused on mine.

"I'm sorry, but I don't like you like that. What happened was a result of my being drunk. Man, I'm sorry that it even happened. I'm not gay; if I were, I'd be the first to admit it. I'm very comfortable with my sexuality. Look, I'm sorry if I misled you in any way. Hopefully, we can forget it and move on." I delivered my message clearly; it was unambiguous and told with conviction. I didn't want to give any hope.

Immediately after saying this, I scanned his face to gauge his reaction. Eddie's smile evaporated. His lips closed and tightened upwards, and he moved his right hand towards his face, motioning his index finger along his upper lip and rubbing his thumb against his chin until both finger and thumb met, pulling his lower lip forward. He said in a low tone, "Okay, I'm sorry. I feel like a fool. If you don't mind, I need to get back to the office."

After those words, we parted ways. I stayed and finished my coffee while he returned to the office. A feeling of dread came over me. I felt like I had ended our friendship and that maybe he'd stop talking to me or lose interest because I told him I wasn't gay.

The next day, we had a new team member start work. I volunteered to walk her around the office and introduce her to people from different divisions within the organization. Our offices occupy three floors. I worked on the first floor and Eddie on the third. When we reached Eddie's floor, my first stop was his desk, but he wasn't there. So, I took her around the floor and came across him in one of the glass conference rooms. He was in a meeting with another team member. I knocked to enter. Eddie nodded his head for me to come in. Without thinking, I blurted, "Damn, you look good." He did. Eddie had a great sense of style. He wore a cement-gray suit with a white shirt and sky-blue tie. He greeted us with a smile, introduced himself and his team's work, and wished us luck as we continued our tour. When I returned to my desk, I grabbed my phone and asked Eddie if he'd be interested in drinks after work that Friday. Immediately, I saw the dots along my screen. They stopped for a minute and then flashed again until I received: *Sure, I'm down.*

Friday came. We started the night grabbing drinks after work at a pub near the office and later transitioned to a bar in Williamsburg near my apartment. We kept our conversation light, discussing work-related topics, then moving to current events, politics, pop culture, and future travel. Neither of us wanted to mention the kisses, coffee, or anything. I hoped that we could move on and hang out. Maybe even not take that or ourselves so seriously.

Eddie took himself seriously, and I had mixed feelings about it. On the one hand, I liked the freedom of talking with him because no topics were off limits—especially about some serious things happening in my life. My relationship with my family, girlfriends—work. I could also share what I felt about something, which I couldn't do with most, really, anybody. But I wished he'd live in the moment a little and not attribute so much meaning to things. Just allow things to happen, chuck it up to the moment, and not always associate it with a hard truth. I liked him, and yes, I was semi-curious about a sexual experience, but I am not gay, nor do I want to be in a gay relationship.

However, tonight Eddie seemed to be on the same page as me—light-hearted, carefree, open—and I was glad for it. I enjoyed the sight of Eddie dancing. Especially when a song came on that he liked. His entire body moved, his arms, chest, hips, and feet fully engaged. He was smooth and rugged, grabbing the attention of others on the floor and pulling them into his sphere of influence. I felt comfortable letting loose with Eddie, not standing on the sideline with my drink in hand, watching out for girls to flirt with, but forgetting the politics of male and female interaction and just having fun with my friend, being present and in the moment.

As usual, I drank a little too much. I must have had five or six drinks that night. It was 3:00 am, and Eddie decided it was time for him to go home. We walked out of the bar together, and without thinking, I playfully kissed him again on the side of his neck. This time he kissed back. I pulled him closer to me. I could feel his penis hardening. We rubbed against each other for a short time. He grabbed my butt and mentioned that it felt hard. I laughed and said, "Gay guys and butts." We rubbed against each other more, and I said, "Alright, it's time to go, Eddie," and he let go.

8

Closer

Several months passed after Alan and I felt each other up that night outside his apartment. The memories of that moment live rent-free in my mind; it was akin to the feeling of hearing the horn blast before a race. Adrenaline rushed through my system, blood traveling from the heart to my external limbs, warming and energizing the points of contact where my body met his. I was grateful that my body was in tune with my desire to feel and instinctively act. With each kiss, rub, and touch, I felt the pulse of my blood underneath my skin. My hands worked, diligently scoping the landscape of Alan's body, and purposefully and with a solid grasp found and clenched his ass. I felt the muscle under my hands contract, squeezing and at the same time gently appreciating feeling his muscles work too, contracting and releasing. Our closeness allowed me to capture his smell. There was a faint scent of spice, likely radiating from the deodorant from his armpits. But what I enjoyed most was our manhoods rubbing against each other, also flush with blood.

That singular incident commenced a new phase in our relationship. Alan and I existed within a gray zone. We routinely spent one-on-one time with each other. We even met outside the confines of our coffee dates, where we'd typically grab drinks at bars or I'd visit him at his apartment. Occasionally, we went to the gym together, with me marveling at his muscular lower half, hoping he'd invite me over afterward, directing me to rub his shoulders, and if I was lucky, giving me a glimpse of his body as he took off his clothes before me to shower. During the warmer months, we'd picnic at the park together. He'd bring wine, a blanket, and a portable speaker, and we'd sit for hours as I listened to the monologue about his future goals and aspirations. We created a world separate from the reality that governed the one outside those four walls. In that space, we could be intimate—kind to each other, share our deepest thoughts, and touch affectionately. Alan would often grab his guitar and sing. Admittedly, he wasn't very good. He'd often alter his voice like Kermit the Frog, but I encouraged him nonetheless because I liked seeing him vulnerable. Each inter- action and meeting in that space contributed to my emotional connection with Alan, and one specific event multiplied the weight, compounding my feelings akin to having an elephant suddenly resting on my shoulders.

But, immediately after the night of our first honest and mutual intimate encounter, I was high on lust. This memory fluttered through my mind this morning as I traveled on the number two train from Brooklyn and got off at the Lower Manhattan Fulton Street stop. I walked through the maze of stairs and escalators, past the passersby, street vendors, and fundraisers, until I made it outside. I tightened my scarf and pulled my jacket closer as I briskly walked to the office. With each breath, I released a condensed cloud that lingered around my face before rising to the sky. My nose hairs instantly froze when I stepped outside.

I forgot my earmuffs and immediately regretted it, feeling my ears burn. My eyes began to tear, too, as I continued my walk to the office, carefully avoiding the motorized bikes that buzzed by, cutting through the cold. The people around me, though diverse, were monochromatic in their appearance, a mix of black, brown, and gray. However, the occasional break of a tartan plaid scarf served as a reminder of the holiday season.

Relief struck as I entered the building. Finally escaping the cold, it was safe to loosen my garments, after which I headed to the security gate, taking note of the giant Christmas tree in the lobby covered in gold tinsel and large round red ornaments. Nearby, at a smaller scale, was inclusive iconography representing both Hanukkah and Kwanzaa. I greeted the security guard and scanned my ID at the electronic gate. I then met a group at the elevator and engaged in the typical morning small talk. I walked into the elevator with them and pushed the button for my floor.

Reaching my desk, I noticed a small Kraft paper card on top of a present wrapped with a repeated snowmen motif and a paste-on red bow. I opened the card first, curious who'd sent it. It read *Eddie* on the cover, written in cursive. I turned the card over and opened the seal held in place by a golden sticker. The envelope was lined with a bright Kelly green and an image of red and white Christmas garland on white string. I pulled the card out of the envelope and admired its quality. On the cover was a small cut-out Christmas tree with red and white felt balls, pine cones with glitter, and a burlap sack with a little tie at the tree's bottom. Red paper lined the inside of the card, with text printed in gold that read: *A very merry wish for a wonderful Christmas.* And directly below this text was a message from Alan. *For all the times you catch the things that others miss. I appreciate you so much for it—Alan.*

I just stared at the card, the words, the packaging. I could feel my eyes well, my vision blurred by the tears ready to spill over. The only thing that snapped me out of it was my cube mate asking me what was inside the package. I reluctantly opened it before her, hoping it wasn't too personal or anything I'd have to explain. I removed the paper wrapping and uncovered a book about street graffiti.

Anytime Alan and I hung out, I'd comment on the public art I noticed in our surroundings, specifically graffiti art. I remember distinctly walking past what I believed to be a Banksy. I commented on it and said, "Art makes everything better." When I opened the book, the inside cover read, *Here's to making things better.*

***

Life was getting better for me. My former boss, Nia, left the corporation, and my unit was restructured with her departure. My new supervisor was a white dude that I got along with a lot better, and on top of that, I was promoted and received a nice bump in pay, which enabled me to leave my apartment and get a place on my own. I found a studio apartment blocks away from Eddie, who helped me secure the place. To rent there, I needed to submit an application and get two references. Of course, I asked Eddie to write me a letter.

To Whom It May Concern,

I've known Alan for the past two years. We met as colleagues but quickly became fast friends. Alan manages a program to support worker cooperatives. When I first met Alan, I was heartened by his passion for the program and eagerness to learn and grow professionally. I was struck by his dedication to his work, and the pursuit of excellence became the foundation of our friendship. Over time, I began to see and learn more about him.

Beyond work, Alan is community oriented. He is involved in various organizations to support voting and civic engagement in North Brooklyn. He participates in youth mentorship programs and volunteers at the local food co-op. On a lighter note, Alan is also a talented guitarist and cook. I've enjoyed a handful of nights with him at his former apartment, listening to him sing, and I can attest firsthand that he's an excellent cook.

Alan is a close friend. He's added value to my life, and I know he'll do the same as a tenant of your co-op.

All the best,

Eddie Adenjj

In the spring, I started seriously dating this girl named Jennah. We first met on New Year's Eve. She was a friend of a friend who came to a gathering I hosted with my roommates. She was one hundred percent my type. A brunette; I fucking love brunettes. Growing up, I had a thing for Mila Kunis types—small, slim girls with dark round eyes and chocolate brown hair. I liked that she was artsy too. Jennah worked as a photographer for a boutique marketing firm. And, last but most importantly, she was great in bed. Very pliable, catering to my needs, and willing to do what I wanted.

Jennah and I had fun. During the summer, we went to a number of music festivals. I remember when we went to an EDM festival at the Ford Amphitheater in Coney Island; she surprised me with tickets to the two-day weekend event where some of my favorite DJs were playing. That Saturday, we went to the beach. The heat that day was unreal; it must have been over ninety degrees. We'd spent most of the day smoking pot, and between puffs, we'd sip our cans of spiked seltzer or cool off in the murky ocean water. We stayed out on the beach for most of the day and transitioned to the festival late afternoon. Jennah looked great—her skin tanned from the sun, her hair in two braids; she effortlessly transitioned from beach to party mood, wearing a mesh top over her swimsuit top and cut-off jeans over her swimsuit bottoms. She painted her face with neon yellow and green right before we took MDMA pills entering the festival. We danced to the music that night, lost in a trance; it was sweaty ecstasy. So, towards the end of summer, I was excited to continue the fun with her and David, my best friend from high school, who had recently moved to Colorado.

David invited me to visit him and join his friends at another EDM festival. It was supposed to be a boys' trip, but naturally, I wanted to invite Jennah. So, I did. I figured David would be cool. He usually was, and his philosophy was the more, the merrier. David loved a party, maybe a little too much. He had hard party habits. When David picked us up from the airport, his eyes darted between me and Jennah. Driving to his place, he looked at me and Jennah more than he did the road—talking excitedly about the wonders of Denver, all the while sniffing his nose and rubbing it at random with the back of his hand. I noticed the signs. He must have done coke before picking us up. I could tell that Jennah was nervous, but she played it cool.

When we got to David's house, he had a few other friends playing video games on an oversized black leather couch, smoking pot. The place was sparsely decorated. A bookshelf was next to the TV, which was on a low-profile TV stand, with a tall floor lamp beside it. Flanking the sofa were two recliners and an oversized gray beanbag. Behind the couch was a low half wall with a countertop and four counter stools.

"Can I get you two something to drink?" David asked as we got deeper into the space.

"Sure, I'll have a beer. Jennah, do you want anything?" I asked her with a smile. She looked back at me and shrugged, nodding her head. "Make that two," I said quickly.

"Sweet! Oh, you can put yourselves in my room. I'll sleep on the sofa."

Before grabbing the beers, we went to his room to drop off our stuff. Its furnishings reflected the living room. Bare, with little personality other than a few photos of his family on top of his chest of drawers. The bed was covered by a navy blue comforter with two flat pillows underneath. We put our luggage near the side of the bed and headed back to the main room to join the others.

Honestly, looking back on that weekend, it wasn't great. The vibe was off with David and with me and Jennah. I remembered David differently growing up. He was down to do whatever—go to parties, listen to the same music, play video games, talk about girls—we spent all our time together. David was famous at school; everyone wanted to know and be him. He threw the best parties and had the most incredible parents. His life was perfect. Now, he appeared haggard with a thinning hairline and a gut, no doubt from all the beer he consumed.

We never spoke about deep shit, but we were comfortable being around each other, even existing silently together. Before we went off to college, we spent that summer and flowed out to California and drove down the highway together—I've always wanted to recreate that experience. However, he changed. He got deeper into drugs and hanging out with people who were into drugs. I liked drugs, but not as much as him. Seeing him like this felt strange, and with these people, it was as if I didn't know him anymore.

Jennah and I had several weird moments. She'd say one thing, but her mood and energy showed another. I was tired the first night and hadn't seen David in over two years, so we stayed home the first night, ordered food, and chilled. Jennah, normally super talkative, remained quiet for most of the night. When we finally went to bed, she started pushing herself on me—I was tired and refused. She pulled the same thing while we were at the festival; we separated from the group and walked around the grounds. She kept trying to push herself on me in the crowd; it was embarrassing. We later got into our first fight. Jennah said that I never considered her needs and that she was constantly bending to me; she wanted me to do things for her and make her feel good when she wanted. The whole thing truthfully confused me. I wanted a good trip, and the two people I was most excited to be with disappointed me.

9

Compartmentalization

During my meditation, I hear the hum of a cell phone vibrating somewhere in the nearby vicinity. I triangulate the source to Elena's purse under the console table. She notices, too, lets go of my hands and says, "I'm sorry, but I have to check my phone. I don't normally answer calls, but my seven-year-old son is ill. I'm coordinating with my mother to pick him up from school. That's probably her calling now. Please continue to focus on what you'd like us to discuss. It will help me to read your future better. This call will only take a moment." She pushes her chair back and rises from the table. Retrieving her phone from the purse, she answers, speaking in a foreign language while exiting the room. I do as she said, attempting to focus on my future, but it's a disingenuous effort. For it was the past that brought me here. It's unresolved; I need a resolution. So, I do the opposite of what she said. I sit there in the haze of smoke from the incense, opening compartments in my mind to uncover the secrets that brought me here today.

***

Alan started a new relationship with a girl called Jennah during the summer of the second year I knew him. I learned about the relationship on our way to the beach. En route, in his car, Alan casually mentioned that he and Jennah had decided to make it official and become girlfriend and boyfriend. Immediately following the statement, there was an awkward silence—only broken by my clearing my throat and saying, "Congratulations, tell me about her. I feel like there is so much that I don't know, like how did you two meet? What does she do? Where does she live?" The barrage of questions continued until we reached the beach. With bright eyes, a big smile, and frequent head nods, I feigned interest in his responses, but deep down, I couldn't help but wonder where this left me. Alan mentioned that he was dating but never gave specifics. It was as if he was passing the time until we could get together, or so I thought. One thing became apparent during the two years I came to know Alan. The women in his life were like toys, shiny playthings that brought him joy, but only for a short time. Eventually, he would get bored and seek something else to entertain him. At first, it alarmed me. "Alan, you must consider their feelings; love how you want to be loved," I would say to him, but my words were hollow, lacking substance. I couldn't hold him to truths that weren't practiced. Slowly, I realized this and that, ironically, I was also a toy for him. My luster would fade. Alan's relationship confronted me with this reality. I chose to ignore the red flags because the value of his choosing to spend time with me outweighed the value I held for myself. I saw the trap, pulled back taut with its numerous triangle-pointed teeth, ready to strike, trapping its next victim, yet I willingly put my hands in. Reality hit, and the sparks of jealousy ignited in me, which undoubtedly would emerge into a full fire in time.

Alan invited me to his apartment for dinner and to watch a movie. He cooked a salmon dish over rice and bought two bottles of orange wine. We planned to watch a sci-fi flick, but after dinner, Alan proposed a romantic comedy he had recently started. I sat on the couch, and he followed with two glasses of wine filled to the rim. He gave me my drink and sat beside me. Fifteen minutes into the show, he moved closer to me. Our thighs touched, and I rested my head on his shoulders. We sat like this for hours. During that period, I moved one leg between his, and he moved his arms around me periodically to strengthen his grip. Occasionally, I'd stare up at him, but his face was fixed on the screen. When it was time to leave, we hugged for a long time, grinding against each other, me gripping his backside and rubbing my face along the side of his. I wanted more; I wanted him sexually, but I was afraid to ask for it directly. Alan gave me enough to keep returning but not enough to soothe my growing desire. Still, I kept my frustration to myself. I did not want to jeopardize the potential of what could happen.

So, when he shared that he was in a relationship, my heart stopped. What did that mean for us and the work I put in to get closer to him, to build trust that he could experiment with me, that I could be what he wanted? It is funny how I compartmentalized this lust for Alan and maintained my relationship with Jacob. It was absurd. I had someone in my life that loved me freely, played no games with sex or intimacy of any kind, who was consistent and made it clear how he felt about me and what he wanted for us in the future. And, although I loved and cared for Jacob, I separated our worlds with the aid of selfish desire and, unbeknownst to me at the time, low self-esteem. I craved Alan's validation; he confirmed my worthiness as someone to be desired and wanted. Alan was a drug; his approval was a drug, and the idea of him choosing me to be the first man he would have sex with was a drug. I was too deep in my addiction, a bona fide addict, so I made the necessary arrangements to ensure a steady supply. Even if it meant lying to Jacob about who I was hanging out with or fabricating lies about train delays, long work hours, and happy hours, I would do anything to keep my fix, which was the imperfect symbolic world I was building in Alan's studio apartment.

***

I got to take a piss. I look around, but there's no portapotty in sight. So, I run off the trail and walk through the woods until I find a relatively private forested area to take a leak. I stop, untuck my penis, and let go. In the process, I check my phone to see the time and if I've received any messages. It's noon, and I don't have any messages. I unzip the pocket over my butt to put the phone back inside and continue onto the path and on my journey.

It was my birthday weekend. Jennah rented a house in Bed-Stuy for us to stay in for three days. For one night, I made plans to invite friends over to celebrate. I asked David to stay with us for the weekend and, for the night, I invited college and work friends to join us for dinner, orchestrated by me. I planned the meal based on recipes from *The New York Times*. I envisioned an Italian-style dinner with homemade bread and gourmet ingredients such as tomato sauce, meats, and the pasta and cheese purchase for the lasagna to be picked up from Whole Foods or places like the West Village's Murray's Cheese. I wanted to impress and was eager to show off my cooking prowess.

The night of, I was stoked to have everyone there to celebrate my birthday, but things were shaky between Jennah and me. Here's the thing, she offered to pay for the weekend but later reneged when she found out the number of people I'd invited; we had different definitions of what a small gathering was. I think she thought it would just be less than five people; I distinctly remember telling her I wanted to have more friends and try my hand at cooking dinner for a large group. I said I wanted David to be there, and I brought up the idea of inviting Eddie, who she'd met a month ago, over pizza. She said something like "the more the merrier" and that she didn't have objections to a few more friends. With her blessing, my list grew to twenty people. I was super excited when I shared the final guest count a few days before the party and was ready for us to start planning. Out of the blue, she asked me to help pay for food and alcohol, which I thought wasn't cool. I mean, I wouldn't have asked her to pay if I was treating her for her birthday.

The party started at 8:00 p.m., but most guests arrived well past 9:00 except Eddie, who came at 8:00 sharp. I asked people to get to my house by 8:45 p.m. when I planned to serve dinner. Unfortunately, that didn't happen. We sat down to eat closer to 9:45 p.m. By then, the lasagna had come out of the oven; it was overcooked but otherwise nearly perfect. Eddie was the first to comment positively on the taste of the food. Beyond the lasagna, he noticed the effort I'd put into everything else. Eddie commented on the bread I'd made from scratch, asked about the ingredients and recipe I used to make the lasagna, and after my birthday song, he praised the tiramisu I'd made. He gave me what I didn't get from my other friends, which I appreciated.

Eddie helped manage the flow of the party through the entire night. While we waited to eat, he poured drinks and directed people to the charcuterie board I had created. In the corner of my eye, I watched Eddie circulate, conversing with everyone. For a moment, I focused on Eddie's interaction with David. Strategically, I leaned against the wall opposite them as they spoke. Eddie must have stood talking with David for at least fifteen minutes. David shared about his life in Colorado and our childhood friendship. He even shared the antidote about the night my dad busted me for attending the party in the woods. The clarity of Eddie's superpower, which set others at ease and facilitated sharing, became transparent to me that night; it was the main reason I loved him. I wanted Jennah to be more like Eddie in this way.

However, Eddie's approach to meeting new people contrasted sharply with Jennah's, who remained insular throughout the night, only engaging with me and barely with David or my other friends. Eddie managed to get her out of her shell at one point in the night. At dinner, we discussed our favorite songs growing up. Jennah was quiet for most of the conversation. I glanced at Eddie, whose eyes were fixed on Jennah. During a dip in the discussion, Eddie asked Jennah, "Of course, these guys are quick to share their favorite bands—but, Jennah, I'm curious. Who were you listening to growing up? Do you have a favorite band or musician?"

Jennah had been moving her food around her plate but stopped after hearing the question. She put her fork down and said, "I liked Taylor Swift. I feel like we grew up together, and because of that have always been able to relate to her music; each of her albums spoke to where I was in my life. I connected with her when she released Fearless. I had that album on repeat. Ever since I've enjoyed seeing her grow as an artist, I feel she's done it right." After that brief interjection, she remained relatively quiet for the rest of the evening.

Eddie and most of my coworkers left around midnight. Once they were gone, the party drugs came out. David brought molly and cocaine and shared them liberally amongst the remaining six. Jennah chose to stay home and sleep while we left to party more in Bushwick. David and I didn't return until 7:00 a.m. and crashed hard most of Saturday into Sunday. Immediately after David left for the airport, Jennah and I argued. She felt I had ignored her for most of the weekend, and I thought she was too needy and didn't engage with my friends. We both got into a shouting match and left each other with the argument unresolved. Monday came, and I felt terrible about how things ended. Throughout the workday, I thought about the fight and planned a text apologizing for how I made her feel. I had drafted a message to send to her, but before I could send it, I received a short email from Jennah that read:

Alan –

I haven't felt good about our relationship for a long time now. You don't appreciate me or respect my time. We've had issues with you constantly showing up late, ignoring text messages, and your lack of curiosity about who I am. I've shared my concerns with you; you promise to do better and, a short time after, relapse into similar patterns of behavior.

This weekend, I felt like you took advantage of me. You invited over twenty people and expected me to pay for everything. Never once did you thank me. In fact, you also barely spoke with me. In the end, you made me feel like I didn't matter.

I don't like who I am when I am around you. For this reason, I want to end this relationship. I sincerely hope you find what you're looking for; I don't think it's me. And I deserve better.

Immediately after reading her email, I tried reaching out. I called multiple times, but the phone just rang out. I tried sending her a message on social media, but she had already blocked me. I was upset; I genuinely tried to make the relationship work. The issues she listed in her email weren't new to me, but I thought I was doing better and had progressed in how I treated her and others. Of course, she couldn't see that or acknowledge my progress. Instead, she focused on my mishaps. I needed a break from it all—work, failed relationships, responsibilities, and the cold—so I started looking for escapes to the beach and asked Eddie to come with me.

10

Palm Beach

"Wait, you want to go to Palm Beach...with Alan, just the two of you?"

Jacob asked the question with his eyes narrowed and head cocked over the table as he served the New Orleans-style red beans and rice he'd prepared for dinner.

"Yeah, I'd like to go," I said timidly. Gathering my strength like a ball rolling down the hill, I continued, "Jacob, you know that Alan and I have become close friends. He just broke up with his girlfriend and asked me to join him to take his mind off things. I want to go. I've been a mentor to him. I'm proud of how our relationship has evolved. I think it would be fun to deepen it with a trip. Besides, I really do feel sorry for him. He's been through a lot at work, and with his family. I think he needs a win. Also, it would be nice to escape the cold weather."

I hoped the last part would resonate with Jacob as a scapegoat for my true intention of wanting to go to Florida. After my comments, I inhaled my first mouthful of adzuki beans, rice, and pork and readily scooped my second serving onto my fork. The heat of the Cajun spices and peppers lingered on my tongue with each swallow. In between my hurried bites, I would probe Jacob's face for any indications of agreement.

"Look, I don't begrudge you for having a friendship with Alan or wanting to escape this fucking cold weather, but I barely know him. You've never really introduced him to me, and it feels off that you want to take a four-day trip with someone I don't know," Jacob said with an even tone, grabbing a bottle of red wine, glasses, and a wine opener from the drawer.

"Well, he did come to my birthday party last year, and I invited you to join me a few weeks ago for his birthday party, but you said you didn't want to go. You're constantly turning down invitations to hang out with my friends and coworkers, but I go out of my way with your friends and family. Look—Jacob, I'll just be gone for a few days. Unlike you, who's out of town for weeks." As soon as the words left my mouth, I regretted them. Jacob stopped eating and looked at me momentarily, but it felt like several minutes had passed, just enough time to notice the smell of spices, minced garlic, and ginger permeating the air around us.

Putting his utensils down and grabbing my hand, Jacob softly said, "If it's important to you, I have no issues. I'm asking all these questions because I care. I know I travel a lot for work, and I'm sorry, but I try to prioritize our relationship when we spend time together; I know I can do better. However, I'm trying to build my career and reach the point where I don't have to travel as much and can take the money I've been saving and invest in a home for us. I hope you can see that and that I love you."

With those words, my heart sank. The truth was that Jacob was going against his better instincts. He was right; something was off about my motivation to travel with Alan. It wasn't based on my need to console a friend but rather my desire to be sexual with one. And, even though I had regrets, they were not enough to dampen this desire. I was willing to risk my relationship with Jacob to experience the possibility of intimacy with Alan, which I hoped could be realized through the cover of travel.

Two months later, on the eve of the trip, I found myself lying in bed, restless, next to Jacob. Questions presented themselves on a continuous loop as if watching headlines stream across the screen on a morning news show. I wanted to know if I would finally have sex with Alan and how it would transpire. I hoped that it would happen the first night. I created a fantasy in my mind of how it would come about and how it would feel. I visualized Alan being gentle and sweet. It would start with a hug and move into light to heavy grinding, something I was already used to with him. We would then proceed to uncharted territory, with sweet kisses on the lips and along the side of our necks. My hands would move into his pants. I would caress his penis and unbutton him and undress him. Once we were both undressed, we would lie on the bed, him on top of me, still grinding, but nude, kissing lying down. I'd be reassuring and communicative, letting him know everything he did was right and felt good. Knowing this would be his first time with a man, I would do my best to make it memorable for him. I pictured him cumming first and being satisfied with that. Knowing my time would come, I hoped we'd do it many times, making up for the lost time of wanting. The thoughts of actualizing these desires held me captive that night and throughout my travels the next day until we finally met in Florida. Alan and I took separate flights because I had an in-person work meeting that I couldn't miss.

Just landed, I texted Alan immediately after arriving in Florida. *Awesome, glad you made it*, Alan responded within seconds of my text message.

I could use a drink! Is there anything at the apartment? If not, I'm happy to pick something up, I wrote, knowing that Alan tended to be more affectionate after a few drinks, and I wanted to speed up the intimacy between the two of us.

Nope, I got you covered. I bought vodka and a mixer earlier today. We're fully stocked, my friend.

Great! We're gonna have a good time. I'm excited to see you, I typed, hoping he felt the same.

I'm excited to see you too, buddy. By the way, I met a girl! Her name is Melissa. We were seated next to each other on the plane this morning. She's based in Palm Beach and agreed to show us around. I'm grabbing drinks with her now. Once you drop your stuff off, you can meet us out. I'll send the address soon.

My heart sank. This trip was supposed to be our weekend: no distractions, no girlfriends, no boyfriends, just us. I read the text over a few times and waited twenty minutes after I walked out of the airport to call a car service to take me to the apartment.

Sure, that's fine. I just called a cab. I'll drop my stuff off and see you in a bit. Can you send me the address and code to enter the apartment? Can't wait to see you!

Alan responded with the rental address and entry code and within minutes the cab arrived. Luckily, the driver was not chatty. In a thick Latin accent, he asked me what brought me into town. I replied, "I needed to escape the cold." He shrugged and nodded in agreement and turned up the Latin pop music playing in the background. As we drove, I stared out the window, feeling a combination of emotions. I was excited to be there for four days, ecstatic to share a flat with Alan, and in disbelief that we would sleep together for three nights on the same bed. But I was also upset. Who was this girl that he'd met? Would it lead to something romantic? Did I come all this way to sleep alone while Alan got into a fling with some girl he met on the airplane? I didn't know. I kept telling myself to stop jumping to conclusions, to remain calm, present, to live in the moment, and to let things unfold. Alan always said that I was too future-oriented. He'd often tell me just to let things happen. I assumed that's why we never took it further; it was my fault—I wanted it too bad. Maybe I just needed to take things in stride and play it cool. In that car, my mantra was, "Just have fun, be cool—no expectations. Whatever happens will happen. Just be open, Eddie."

It was close to 10:00 p.m. when I arrived at the apartment. Our rental was on the side of an all-white ranch-style home in a quiet residential neighborhood. When I entered, the studio appeared precisely as shown on the Airbnb posting selected by Alan. There was a small room, only large enough to fit a queen-sized bed. It was set up with all the usual items: a TV mounted on the wall, a dorm-size refrigerator underneath a table with a coffee maker, condiments, paper cups, and two mini bottles of water on top of the desk and chair. On the left side of the wall at the entrance into the apartment was a large wardrobe to hang clothes and place luggage, with a door towards the end of the wall that led into a compact bathroom with a standing shower and a flimsy shower curtain, the kind that always leaks water during prolonged use. There was only one large rectangular window well above the bed's headboard.

I stood at the entrance, frozen, scanning the surroundings. The sight of Alan's laptop and a few other personal belongings on the table got me out of my trance. I entered the space, opened the wardrobe, and saw more evidence that he had been there. Alan's clothes were neatly hung on hangers inside, his large duffle bag on the bottom shelf, and his undergarments folded and organized within the first two drawers as if he were home. Even his smell lingered, something reminiscent of Old Spice. This trip was happening. Alan and I would finally spend uninterrupted time together, or so I hoped. My phone beeped and vibrated, interrupting the silence in the small room. It was a text message from Alan. He shared his location and encouraged me to meet with him and Melissa at a Mexican bar. After washing up, I entered the address in Google Maps and texted Alan that I'd be there in thirty minutes. Ten minutes later, I made my way to meet them.

As I approached the bar, I immediately noticed Alan seated outside. He wore a black t-shirt with the Supreme logo plastered on the front, paired with khaki drop crotch joggers and black Vans. Next to Alan was Melissa. She wasn't what I expected, which was a thin-lipped white woman with longish hair; instead, Melissa was a dark-skinned, athletic black woman with a shaved head and a nose ring. Her eyes were like slanted almonds, and her smile was large, showing off her sparkling white teeth. I could tell she was likely a personal trainer or involved in something sporty. I walked over, gave Alan a hug, and then introduced myself to Melissa. I then asked them both if they wanted drinks, which they declined. I got myself a margarita and went back to them. During our conversation, she revealed that she was a Pilates instructor who often traveled to provide her services at corporate wellness retreats.

There was a casual energy between the two of them that I didn't like; it was as if they had known each other personally for some time. Melissa's hand graced his several times during the conversation, and the volume of her laughter increased exponentially with every remark he made. My interaction with her was civil. I feigned interest in her work and asked probing questions about her life in Palm Springs, hoping that she would disclose that she had a boyfriend or describe some romantic entanglement, but nothing to my satisfaction manifested. Instead, she seemed intent to continue gushing over Alan, and he was more than happy to indulge her.

We reached a stalemate by night's end. It was 2:00 a.m. The bar had already stopped serving alcohol, and our cups had stood empty on the table for the past forty-five minutes. At this point, Melissa was clearly searching for new conversation starters. I did my best to appear engaged, smiling and nodding to show that I was listening and, at the same time, sneaking glances at Alan to measure his mood. Alan was the one to call it a night. We paid our bill and exited the premises. Before we left, I used the restroom, partly because I had to go but also because I wanted to give Alan and Melissa some privacy before we departed. When I came back, she was giving him an intimate hug, with her arms around his neck, and he was rubbing her back. I felt sick—was he going to leave with her? Before I could ask, Alan spoke.

"Hey there, Eddie. Melissa lives in the opposite direction of us, so we'll say goodbye now, but she wants to hang out with us tomorrow night. What do you say?" He asked in front of her, knowing I wouldn't say no.

"Of course, we should hang out again," I said, mustering all the excitement I could.

Alan smiled, put his hand over my shoulder, and we returned to the rental together.

When we got back, I immediately went to wash up, and Alan crashed on the bed with his shoes still on, turning on the television, navigating to Netflix, and watching movie previews. In the bathroom, I brushed my teeth, washed my face, and feverishly used the washcloth to freshen up my underarms and private parts. I quickly changed into my pajamas and opened the door to see Alan moving a mini bottle of water from his mouth to the bedside table, still awake. I opened the wardrobe to put my clothes away and started to talk about Melissa.

"Melissa seemed nice and friendly, but also overly talkative—I don't think I got more than a sentence out at a time while talking with her. What are your thoughts about her?" I asked him, curious if this was a romantic connection or just something to pass the time while he was waiting for me to arrive.

"I don't know, man, she's cool. Plus, it's nice that she's local. Maybe she can show us more of the area." Alan said this while looking at the screen, still flipping through the viewing options.

I followed up, seeking to change the subject. "I'm just happy to be here and finally spend one-on-one time with you. We've been discussing this trip for months, and here we are."

Alan stood up, wrapped his arms around me, and rubbed my back like with Melissa. Usually, I'd wait until he pulled me into his body to reciprocate, but I was too excited. I also lifted my arms to rub his back and voluntarily moved my right leg into his groin. We rubbed against each other for a few minutes, and when I moved to kiss Alan's neck, he said, "Let's get some sleep. It's late, and I'm tired. I promise we have the rest of this week and the weekend."

Reluctantly, I let go. I got into bed and did my best to sleep that night.

***

I was excited to have Eddie join me in Palm Springs. I'd tried to organize a group trip before with two other friends, but I couldn't make it across the finish line. Initially, I wanted to go to Turks Caicos. I brought the idea up with Eddie, who immediately responded yes, and then I reached out to David and another friend, who were both on the fence. David wanted to go to Puerto Rico, which didn't interest me—and my other friend was just flaky. I ended up booking the trip to Turks Caicos with just me and Eddie, but I had to rethink the trip's timing because it was happening at the same time as my grandparents' seventieth wedding anniversary. When I looked at tickets and lodging again, the prices had increased, so I decided for us to go to Palm Springs.

I don't have a good explanation for why I chose a one-bed Airbnb rental for Eddie and me to share. Maybe I was curious. It was no secret that we had a special friendship; I felt comfortable around him. I didn't want to have sex per se, but I liked his attention and knew I had control of the situation. Nothing would happen unless I let it.

I overdrank the night before, and waking up the next day was a challenge because I didn't get enough sleep. That night, while Eddie was sleeping, I was still watching TV. Something in me felt restless. I eventually dozed off around five-ish and barely slept four hours, which wasn't the best circumstance, considering I had to work the next day. I didn't fully wake up until 10:00 a.m., causing me to miss my 9:15 check-in with my boss. Eddie tried waking me up, but apparently, I got up temporarily at 9:00 and then immediately fell back to sleep after he left to give me space to work. Eddie decided to explore the downtown area and read on the beach. I emailed my boss, apologizing and explaining that I had felt ill and needed to take the day off. There would be repercussions, but the damage was already done.

After emailing my manager, I closed my laptop, grabbed my phone, and texted Melissa.

Hey there, beautiful. Let's meet up today at the beach. When are you off work?

Good morning! I could meet you at Lake Worth Beach at five. Does that work for you?

Let's meet early, say four. I'll text my homie and have him meet us, too.

OK, I should be able to leave a bit earlier. I'll bring a girlfriend along to join us. See you later

***

To kill time that day while Alan worked, I went sightseeing and ate lunch on my own. Around 3:30 p.m., I returned to the Airbnb, only to find Alan getting ready to meet up with Melissa.

"Hey man, how was your day?" Alan said in an upbeat mood, clearly well rested.

"It was good. I ended up visiting the Johnson History Museum. I saw—"

"Right on! Glad you had fun. I'm on my way to meet Melissa and her friend. Let's talk about your day on the way to the beach?" he said with a smile, unaware of my internal annoyance.

"Well, I just got back. How about I meet you...and your new friend...there? I want to rest up," I said, unable to contain my disappointment.

"Oh...oh, yeah, that's cool—but don't rest too long, man. We're on vacation; all we're doing is relaxing on the beach. Promise me you won't stay here by yourself. Besides, we got to maximize our time together," Alan said, softening his tone, smiling visibly with his teeth and eyes.

"Yeah, yeah. I'll likely be there soon. I want to make a call, but I'll see you shortly." My annoyance disappeared and was replaced with hopefulness—Alan wanted me there, I knew. I just needed to be cool.

I arrived at the beach an hour later, fifteen minutes before sunset. Alan, Melissa, and her friend were lying on a blanket and smoking pot.

"Hey, Alan. Hi, Melissa, it's good seeing you again." I gave Alan a warm hug and Melissa a semi-friendly handshake. My words couldn't be further from the truth, but I had to play it cool. The last thing I wanted was to appear like I couldn't go with the flow. I wanted Alan to see me as spontaneous and ever-present, always up for adventures in whatever form they appeared. Besides, I hoped this agreeable attitude would win me points, a currency he would count and determine when I had accrued enough to cash in on complete intimacy with him. Now, through self-examination, I realize that this behavior was manipulative. I sought to influence Alan, similar to the ways that I tried to get those school kids to like me by bringing candy every day on the playground years ago. It was my default, a habit I groomed over time through practice and reinforced with each reward.

After our greetings, we all remained standing to view the sunset. Melissa's friend, Lexie, handed me a joint to enhance the moment. I'm not much of a smoker. I can count on one hand the number of times I've tried and how the experiences backfired on me. Still, I was playing it cool and attempted it, only to commence a horrible coughing spell, which disrupted the serenity of the waves of the ocean cascading to the shore, the humid breeze brushing against our skin, and the fading rays of the sun, hues transitioned from gold to pink, and pale blue to purple across the sky. I was trying to be cool but was hyper-aware of myself, so much so that in conversation with

Melissa, I came out because, maybe subconsciously, I needed to explain why I was so awkward in their presence, and my being gay somehow was the perfect explanation. She stared back at me blankly and said, "I figured you were," and exhaled, pushing the smoke towards the direction of the water.

We parted ways around 7:00 p.m. and agreed to meet again around 11:00 p.m. at a club downtown. In between, Alan and I grabbed dinner along the waterfront and headed back to our apartment to rest up, shower, and change. Walking back to the unit, I mustered up the courage to share that I didn't want to hang out with Melissa for the entire trip. We planned this trip to spend time together, but so far, most of the time was spent with Melissa, and I felt like a third wheel. Alan, per usual, found the right words, saying, "I'm sorry. I can see how you'd feel that way. We'll spend the entire day together tomorrow—just the two of us. I want us to go to John D. Macarthur State Beach. I've seen pictures, and it's beautiful; we'll get high together and chill."

***

I hadn't brought much to wear to go to the club. Eddie was cool enough to let me borrow a shirt. When we entered the club, the bouncer validated what I already knew: that I looked sharp. It was packed when we arrived. I grabbed a beer and bought Eddie an old-fashioned one. Melissa and Lexie were still on their way, so Eddie and I took our drinks to the floor and danced. One thing that I love about Eddie is that when he's not in his head, he can let loose, and it's contagious. He attracted this group of three girls who started to dance with him. They were a little too young for my taste, most likely in their late teens or just twenty, but hot nonetheless. One of them caught my eye. She was a fit brunette with nice pale skin. I don't care about breast size, but I like fit girls. We had a short exchange as we danced. We danced for over thirty minutes. I didn't realize that Melissa and Lexie arrived until Eddie tapped my shoulder to tell me. I was dancing with the brunette in the pink skirt for too long, making Melissa uncomfortable to approach. I laughed it off and bought us all another round of drinks. Melissa forgot about it soon enough, and we all had a good time.

At one point in the night, I motioned Eddie to dance with me and Melissa. He was off alone when the group of girls left, and I wanted to make sure he felt included. I'd had four beers and was feeling good. The back of my shirt was soaked. Melissa noticed and unbuttoned the front button. I oscillated between Eddie and Melissa with each song or changed in between. I was gyrating with her between my thighs and swinging to Eddie with my hands grasping his shoulders for reassurance. I only took breaks for a quick smoke or drink run; each took turns accompanying me. Before the night ended, I felt like I'd established my territory with paths to facilitate my needs: bathroom, drinks, smoke, and back to Melissa and Eddie. By night's end, I was ready to blaze a new path, feeling adventurous. Her friend Lexie, left us earlier in the night. I asked Melissa if she wanted to come back to our apartment to continue the fun, and she said yes. So, I hailed a cab, and all three of us got in.

I knew what Eddie wanted. He wanted us to have sex. I wasn't comfortable with it just being the two of us, but I thought we could add a third. I never shared this plan with him. I'm not sure I knew this would be the plan, but I wanted to have this experience, and I couldn't think of a better person to have it with than Eddie. However, I miscalculated. I thought Melissa would be down, but she wasn't. When we returned to the apartment, she saw only one bed. I eased the tension, poured the three of us drinks, and then called her to the bed to start making out. Eddie sat in the chair, frozen. I motioned him over, and she objected, saying, "I only want it to be us. I'm not into that."

I continued to kiss her, saying, "Okay."

Eddie remained frozen in the chair, watching. I pulled off my shirt, and she stopped again.

"You don't have another bed or space? This setup feels strange. Aren't you uncomfortable with your friend watching us? I'd prefer to be outside, please."

"Sure, no problem." I put my shirt back on and walked her outside, where a bench was just outside our door, and we continued to make out. According to her, Eddie watched through the window, and she still felt uncomfortable. She asked if we could go back to her place. I didn't want to go. Truthfully, I wasn't attracted to her enough to want to make the connection happen. After ten minutes of making out on the bench, she left, asking if we could connect tomorrow. I said, "Sure, let's play it by ear."

When I came into the room, Eddie was lying in bed. He stood to hug me. I remember hugging him back and going to bed.

***

It was early morning, around 6:00 a.m., when I was awakened. Alan had his left leg around me. His lips pressed against my neck, and his groin slowly rubbed against my ass. His left arm weaved between my arm and torso, with his hand resting on my chest. I was paralyzed, exhibiting no signs of life—like a possum, playing dead, afraid to move. I wasn't sure what was happening. My mind raced as I waited for another sign or action from him to provide more information. And, as if he read my mind, it happened: Alan started rubbing his feet against mine. I remained still. His movements continued; his thighs rubbed against mine in tandem with his groin, and like a jolt of electric current, I felt him harden, pushing more rigorously against me. I remember the heat of his breath on my neck, the tingle I experienced from his lips, and the nudge of his nose—the sensation of the rubs felt gentle, soft, and sweet. These actions continued for several minutes until I finally dared to react. As he moved his groin against me, I moved in countermotion to create friction. However, after several minutes, he stopped and rolled over to his back.

I stayed on my side for a minute, maybe two, and decided to roll over to my back. Mustering courage, I tilted my head towards him; he was smiling. I quickly looked upward, afraid to view his face again, and instead let my hand move up and down his chest. I peeked again and saw that the smile remained. I grew bolder. I shifted my hand from his chest to his penis. I began gently massaging it, starting with the outline of the tip and moving up and down the end and along the shaft to his ball sack. Initially, I performed the caressing motion over his underwear but quickly progressed to his naked penis. I continued until my fingers felt the discreet secretion of precum. I looked at my fingertips and then at him and decided to kiss him. I leaned over, pressed my lips against his, and our eyes locked.

With a surprised look, Alan exclaimed, "Whoa, whoa, whoa. Gay."

I was shocked. I moved my head away and sat upright. My mouth opened, but no words came. And, Alan continued, now upright with his back against the headboard.

"I thought you were a girl, man. Not cool. Not cool at all."

He then went back to sleep, lying on his stomach, and started grinding on the bed. I wasn't sure what was happening; I just stared at him in disbelief. The grinding continued for minutes. He got up as if nothing had happened, went to the toilet, came out, reached for his phone, and got back into bed, sitting upright, and said, "I found another Airbnb closer to Lake Worth; I'm going to book it."

In a panic, I said, "No, I'm sorry. Please don't. I'm sorry, Alan. Our trip can't end like this; I really don't want you to go." I started to cry hysterically, still unclear about what had happened but feeling that I was at fault.

He looked at me the entire time, grabbed his phone, canceled the reservation, and, with a steady voice, said, "Alright, it's okay. I canceled the request. Let's just put this behind us."

"Yes, I agree," I said quickly, following his words, and we honored our agreement for the rest of our trip.

***

I don't remember what happened. I blacked out. All I know is that Eddie tried kissing me. I wasn't in control; I was dreaming and thought he was a girl. It wasn't cool for him to take advantage of me. Anyway, he apologized, and I dropped it. The rest of the trip was cool; no more incidents. We went to Alan D. MacArthur State Park for the day, and I got him to try acid for the first time; it was INCREDIBLE. Eddie had this childlike energy, ha—he was doing cartwheels on the beach, and we got into this dense conversation about urbanism and how it would translate underwater, a modern-day Kingdom of Atlantis. We stretched out, high for hours. In fact, so long that we overstayed park hours. By the time we got back to the park entrance, it was night, and the park ranger had closed the gate. I freaked out; the gate was at least twelve feet tall with spikes on top. Eddie found a section of the gate without spikes, climbed the fence, and jumped over—cheering me on to do the same.

The rest of the night, we laughed about getting high and had wacky conversations—processing his experience of being high and the gate. We were both too tired to do anything else that evening, so we just ordered Mexican food and watched a Netflix documentary about psychedelics. We crashed that night and did it all again, minus LSD, the next day.

Eddie left for the airport first. I was scheduled to leave later that evening. Before he left, we grabbed lunch and walked along the pier of Lake Worth Beach. We hugged when the time came for him to go, and he was off.

Before his flight, Eddie sent me a text with a few photos he had taken of us on the trip.

Hey buddy, thanks again for a great time. I wouldn't change a thing. I appreciate you and love you.

Love you too, homie, great trip! Glad we could make it work. Great photos, too; looking forward to seeing the rest later. Safe travels back to NY!

11

The Breakup

Deep in my meditation, my eyes begin to water, not from the smoke, but from the sad state my life is currently in. I am alone. In a room filled with fantastical images and statues, I am waiting for Elena to guide me to a path of salvation. Yet, she couldn't even foresee her son being ill to compensate for her being late to our appointment. I feel like life is playing a cruel joke on me. It's telling me I don't deserve to feel happy or secure; that no one will ever take me seriously. I feel ready to embrace my insignificance.

***

When I returned home from Palm Beach, adjusting to everyday life was hard. My relationship with Jacob suffered. Everything he did annoyed me. In my mind, I compared him to Alan. Jacob wasn't funny enough. He wasn't adventurous enough. He wasn't passionate enough. I found problems to wedge us apart. I can now admit that I was blinded by my infatuation for Alan, so much so that I overlooked his faults and the reality of our time together, which was made painfully clear because we were never able to discuss the incident in Palm Springs—the night we took our dance around intimacy to the next level. I was in denial that it meant anything more to him than just an experiment gone wrong, and well, I think that he was in denial on his part in the whole thing. I tried to address it with him the handful of times we saw each other but each time I found myself back in that bed that morning in Palm Springs when he first engaged me, paralyzed, waiting for his permission to make a move. I needed him to take the lead and start the conversation. The closest we came to discussing what happened was during a jog through Prospect Park.

Occasionally, Alan and I would jog together. We hadn't done so in a while because of the cold, but it was approaching spring— the weather was starting to warm in parallel to my optimism that I'd finally be able to talk with Alan about our relationship. When we met at the park's entrance, he looked handsome in a long-sleeved running shirt and black tights. It wasn't quite warm enough for his attire, but he never really dressed right for the season; whether it was just a leather jacket in the middle of a blizzard or thick khaki jogger pants in the height of summer, his looks were simply to command a sense of calm.

We hugged as we always do when we meet, and right away, we started to run. Alan was searching for another job and had already interviewed at another organization. He was recapping the interview and seeking my input on his chances. He gave me the play-by-play, I listened while running, and when he looked for me to speak, I shared my feedback while maneuvering the dance of talking and getting enough air to breathe.

After we completed the 3.35-mile loop around the park, we walked onto the Grand Army side at his request to grab a beer and chat further. We took our beers and sat down, and before I could speak, Alan suggested we take another trip, this time to Upstate New York. I was flabbergasted. Alan wanted to do another trip. We had never really processed the last one a month ago; I wasn't sure what the status of our current relationship was, but at the same time, I was hopeful that maybe it was something more than before. I thought perhaps we were breaking through about his sexuality, and if I were patient, I'd be able to help him through coming out, and the payoff would be us being in a relationship together.

"Alan, I'd love to go upstate with you. When do you think we'd go?" I said immediately, surprising myself.

"Sweet, I was thinking in late May or June. I've always wanted to rent a cabin there but never had anyone to do it with. We could get high again, hike, and chill. It'd be great to rent a nice place. Maybe with a hot tub?" Alan said, confident in his vision.

"Yeah, that all sounds great. It may need to be June, though. I'm gonna have to convince Jacob about going on another trip with you," I said with uncertainty, unsure if Alan would care.

There was an awkward moment of silence after that comment. We both took sips of our drink and then Alan said, "Oh, yeah. I see. How's your relationship going? Everything okay?"

"Not really. I'm thinking maybe we should break up. I'm not sure if I'm happy anymore." I wanted to say more. I wanted to tell him that I felt preoccupied with my relationship with him and wanted to help him in his coming out, but I was reluctant. Deep down, I knew that sharing that would scare Alan. Maybe, deep down, I knew it wasn't true for him, but I wanted to hold on to this possibility, in case it was, so I held back.

"Well, you deserve to be happy, Eddie. You're a great guy and should be with someone equally great." Alan smiled at me, finished his beer, and got another. We stayed long after his second drink. He drank his, finished mine, and then we grabbed city bikes home.

That night, Eddie forwarded me an apartment listing that had recently opened up in his co-op. It was a studio apartment located on the floor beneath his unit. The email he sent with the link was brief but instilled hope inside of me. It read:

Hey man,

This apartment is available in my building. If things don't work out with you and Jacob, there are options out there for you to find a new place. Whatever you do, I want you to be happy.

The message from Alan and the surface feelings I conjured up about my unhappiness with Jacob triggered me to act, to move forward with my resolve to break up with Jacob. I didn't process this decision, consider my reasons, or weigh out the pros and cons of my situation. Simply put, I did not understand why I was unhappy with Jacob; we'd been together for six years without incident. I just had a feeling that it wasn't a good fit. Yes, he traveled a lot, but he was good to me when he was around. I knew that he loved me, not only through his words but also through his actions. My relationship with him was easy, too easy. I questioned his love for me; how can he love me for just me and not expect something in return? Deep down, I didn't trust him or the love he claimed to have for me. I may not have consciously known it, but I'd always had one foot in and the other out the door. Love didn't feel real to me without strife. So, when I decided to break up with Jacob, I felt relief. Now, I was free to invest my time to win over Alan.

The breakup happened the day after I received the email from Alan. It was a Friday. I sat at my desk, read his email, and viewed the listing several times. The resolve to leave Jacob simmered slowly at first but quickly boiled over. I went home early that day, gathered my belongings, booked a hotel room, and then waited for Jacob to arrive to tell him in person.

He walked through our front door, passing the galley kitchen and putting his jacket in the hallway closet. He then placed his keys on the sofa table further down the hall and found me on the sofa with my travel bag next to me.

"Hey, babe. What's up?" he said, his voice transitioning from upbeat to questioning after seeing my bag.

"Jacob, I think we should break up." The words just came out. I had nothing planned, no words to cushion the news or a thoughtful explanation of why this was happening. I just spoke and decided to let things transpire as they may.

"What the fuck, Eddie. Is this a joke? You want to break up? Why? What's the reason, and how long have you been thinking about this? What did I do? I thought we were good. Why do it like this, so abruptly with your bags packed like you're leaving an abusive relationship?" Jacob said, anger rising with each question.

I said in a cold, unwavering voice, "I'm just not happy anymore."

The words felt foreign and untrue. I wasn't unhappy with Jacob but had fabricated a fantasy that Alan would fulfill me. Alan was everything I thought I wanted to be: intelligent, handsome, and worthy of admiration. I couldn't explain this logic because it was nonsensical. To leave someone who manifested love for somebody who refused to acknowledge it was absurd. Needless to say, it wasn't surprising that I couldn't explain my actions to Jacob.

"You know what, you're self-centered. That's all you have

to tell me after six years? I've done nothing but give you my best. I loved you the best way I know how. You've given me no indication that you haven't been happy. You haven't given me a chance to fix it. Let's try. What are you unhappy about? Is it my traveling? It feels like you made a decision, but I think we should try to work things out, not throw this relationship away." The anger faded away from his voice, replaced with concern.

"I just need some time to think," I said, my voice lower and the clarity of certainty lost. "I booked a room at a hotel. I'm going to stay there for the time being." I began walking towards the door.

"Eddie, this is incredibly hurtful. I'm shocked. I don't deserve this. I don't deserve to be treated this way. I hope you think long and hard about what you're doing because I will be doing the same." Those were his final words when I walked out the door from my old life and into the new.

I had booked a hotel room in Downtown Brooklyn. Instead of our thoughtfully decorated home in Prospect Heights, I was in a similar space to the one I shared with Alan in Palm Springs, but it felt lonely. I immediately put my things away, grabbed something to eat, and, when I got back, sent a text message to Alan.

Alan, I officially separated from Jacob today. It's been building over time. I needed something big to happen to make it a reality, and that happened for me in Palm Springs. I'm not sure what I want from you, but I thought you should know.

Eddie, I appreciate you sharing and hope you're holding up okay. I know this must be a difficult time and am wishing you all the best. Most importantly, hope you find what you're looking for, buddy. You're a good guy—you deserve it.

I must have read Alan's message twenty times, hoping to

discover something new, a hidden message to help decode his reaction to my newfound availability. I hoped that my declaration of freedom would spark meaningful change. Alan would finally be open to me; he would acknowledge my efforts, come to my hotel room—help me pack up my things, and I'd go back home with him. I envisioned the start of a genuine relationship; life would go on, and I would finally be happy. But that's not what happened. After reading his text message that twentieth time, I felt lonelier than I had before leaving Jacob, before texting Alan, and before I chose to sit in this hotel room alone.

My second communication was with my friend Kenji from back when I lived in New Orleans, who moved recently to Jersey City with a girl he met in school shortly after graduating college. We'd remained loosely connected all these years, communicating through occasional emails or rare phone calls about our progress through the various stages of our lives. Kenji was the only person who knew me before when there was still light in my eyes. It felt comforting to seek his counsel now entirely in the dark.

I sent him a text asking if he was available to talk. He said yes immediately, and I quickly called. I explained the series of events, my breakup with Jacob, and my tenuous relationship with Alan. Kenji listened intently on the other end, confirming his attention with the occasional "yes, I see," and "okay." I sincerely trusted him, and I felt comfortable confiding in him about everything with the exception of Palm Springs. I wasn't ready to share the shame of that experience.

Kenji continued to listen and after I'd exhausted my words on the topic, he made a statement, followed by a question. "It sounds like you have deep feelings for Alan, a high degree of doubt and fear included. Can I ask you something?" He paused, waiting for my response.

"Sure, go ahead," I said.

"How has your relationship with Alan served you?"

At first, I struggled to answer partly because I didn't understand what he meant by the question.

"What do you mean? Are you asking me the reasons I'm continuing to pursue the relationship?" I said with reasons lined up—he's smart, handsome, makes me laugh, and is adventurous.

"No, what I mean is, how does he support you? How does he affirm you? What purpose does this relationship have to make you happy?

"Eddie, I don't know Alan, but you haven't shared anything with me suggesting he contributes to your wellbeing. It sounds like he takes, and you give. That doesn't sound like a healthy relationship to me. It sounds one-sided.

"I hope my words don't come across as too harsh. I care about you, and I want to see you happy with someone that appreciates you. You owe it to yourself to be direct about your needs. If Alan is who you think he is, he'll listen and step up. But, if he's not, he won't. Either way, you deserve an answer. Especially if you're planning to end a relationship with Jacob, someone who by all counts has shown up for you."

A groundswell of emotions rose to the surface after my call with Kenji. Of course, my friend was right. I needed to confront Alan about the nature of our relationship and what happened in Palm Springs—ask him directly if he cared for me in the same way I cared for him. With courage and inspiration at the helm, I poured myself into an email and sent it to Alan that evening.

Dear Alan,

I have enjoyed getting to know you and building our friendship for the past three years. You've shared so much with me about your family and personal life; I'm honored that you've put trust in this relationship.

Over time, we've built a unique intimacy. I've come over to your place many times and enjoyed your company. Listening to you play your guitar, eating food you've prepared from recipes mined from The New York Times, and watching shows, occasionally with my head on your shoulder.

We've embraced each other many times, with you rubbing your body against mine, and on rare occasions, you've kissed me along my neck. We've both shared that we love each other, and I believe we've both meant it.

We've never discussed what happened at Palm Springs, but we should. You attempted a threesome with me, and when it was unsuccessful that morning, you initiated more intimacy by rubbing yourself onto me. I accepted it and was happy to reciprocate.

I need to know what all of this means. Do you want to pursue something more than just a friendship? I do. I care about you, and I want to finally admit it to you. However, I'm confused by everything that's happened. You sent me an apartment listing and have begun to organize another trip for just the two of us. Why?

It hurts that I told you that I left my partner, and you only texted me. I would have done more for you. If I'm honest, I hoped you would have done more, maybe offered to come to the hotel to talk in person.

I guess I'm asking you for clarity on what our relationship means to you because I want more than what I'm getting from you now.

Sincerely,

Eddie

***

I finished my run. Now, I'm stretching, trying to make sure I don't pull a muscle. I have a date scheduled tonight with Tonya, a girl I just started chatting with on Tinder. However, I won't meet her until 8:00 p.m. and it's only 1:00 p.m. now. I could go back home and finish working on my resume and respond to the job posting that David sent me, but I'm not in the mood. Instead, I think I'll grab a beer and drink in the park. It's still early enough. I'm sure my favorite beer shop window will be open by now. Honestly, I want to numb my mind, forget, and relax. But it's hard. I keep thinking about Eddie. I shared a lot with him, and he hurt me. The best thing for me now is to push it all down and forget, but for some strange reason, I can't.

***

I had mixed emotions when I received Eddie's text message that he'd broken up with Jacob. On one hand I was happy for him. He told me that he wasn't satisfied in his relationship. I wanted him to be happy. But, on the other hand, I had a feeling that I might have played a part in his decision.

Look, I'm aware that he had feelings for me and I played into them. I've never experienced relationships with other men like with Eddie. He challenged me emotionally. I never revealed to anyone about my obsessive relationship with my mother or my feelings of abandonment from my father. I felt safe to share with Eddie. Not only that, I started to want him to see me in a positive light. I wanted to be the person he wanted me to be. I think that's why I allowed a discreet amount of intimacy between us. I wanted him to get what I thought he wanted in our relationship. But, things got out of hand, and now we're here.

In my gut, I knew it was time to end the relationship. But this was confirmed when I received his email. There was no right time to do it. I just couldn't shoulder the responsibility of his relationship ending because of me.

So, I took two days to respond to his email. My response was as follows:

Dear Eddie,

I'm sorry I didn't respond to your email right away. I needed some time to process it and come to a decision about our friendship moving forward.

For a long time, you've been one of my closest friends—often the closest. I've enjoyed our happy moments together and the generosity and love you bring to the world. You've inspired me to be a more reflective, considerate person, and in so many ways, I am a better person for having met you.

How much you've given to me is what has made me go back and forth on our friendship many times as I try to understand what I don't like about how you see me. Trying to understand which outweighs the other. How I might be able to keep the good and alter the bad.

What do I mean by the bad? Well, I've had a problem with alcohol ever since I started drinking. I'm unable to stop time after time, and I say and do embarrassing things. More importantly, I always wake up feeling worse because I know I'm not in control; the alcohol is.

Every significant partner and friend I've had has commented

on this, told me I should seek help. Except you. I don't believe it's because you want to hurt me; rather my 'lack of control' offers you moments when you can be intimate with me.

I don't think you seek this out from a 'rape-y' angle. I think you truly believe a part of me—the "truthful" part of me—seeks this. And I don't think there's anything I or anyone else can say that would change your mind.

The truth is that I've had a dysfunctional relationship with sex for a long time. As a kid, locked in my bedroom with violence at my door, I lost myself in porn. Over time, it began to warp what I found sexual, and normal sex became less enjoyable.

I've learned that my sexuality as it relates to men has less to do with men and more with my feelings of insecurity and inferiority. When men appear, they don't have sex with me—they have sex with the women I want. A self-imposed humiliation.

I've never admitted this to anyone because of the shame I feel. But I admit it to you on the chance it helps you understand that sex or a romantic relationship with you or any man is not what I seek. And the fact that you didn't take the time to understand that leaves me more damaged and less trusting of you. You don't always have my best interests at heart, even if you don't know it.

I'm not sure what the outcome of this email will be, but I hope it leads to a greater understanding of me, our friendship, and my honest reasons for closing it. I sincerely wish you all the best, Eddie. I know you are a good guy and were an incredible friend (far better than me) in so many ways, and I hope you continue to give your gifts of love and generosity to all those who deserve it.

I felt relief when I sent the email. I cared about Eddie, but I couldn't take on the responsibility asked of me. I just wanted to have fun. I'll accept my part in leading him on, but I made no promises of love or that our relationship would ever become more serious. I set clear boundaries of what I wanted: just fun. I'm sorry things didn't work out with his partner, but that wasn't my concern.

I heard back from Eddie two hours after I sent my message. I didn't open his email, instead I chose to delete it. I stopped all communication with him and decided to end that chapter.

***

Dear Alan,

Your friendship is important to me. I also consider you my best friend, and I love you so much. I've loved seeing the world through your eyes. You were the person that I wanted to be around the most. Our friendship was complicated, but I've tried to be the person you wanted me to be. I've tried to know and support you and be intimate with you on your terms.

Every chance I got, I asked questions. There was no topic off limits with us; whether they were about your work life, your family, or your relationships—I tried to know you. It is hurtful to hear that you don't think this is true, but I cannot change your perception. However, I want you to know that I did my best.

Alan, you don't have a monopoly on pain. I've experienced pain, doubt, and intense feelings of inadequacy too, but you've never probed these areas with me. At least I tried with you.

And you're right. I noticed your heavy drinking. I agree it isn't healthy. Maybe I should have been more outspoken about it or encouraged you to drink less, but you were more affectionate with me when you drank and I'll admit that I craved intimacy with you. It filled a void in my heart, and I loved the attention you showed me. I admire you and wanted your light to shine in my direction.

I cannot know what I don't know. I didn't understand the extent of your porn addiction or how it was used to soothe you during moments of abuse and violence in your life. For me, what comforted me was the approval of others. I needed to feel loved and liked. I'm not sure entirely why this is important, but it is—rejection hurts, especially coming from you. However, I can't be blamed for things that happened in your past; it's not fair.

I'm sad that the friendship must end. Alan, I had to speak up about Palm Springs. I'm sorry that your interpretation is that I have not taken the time to know you. Again, I've tried, but I need help knowing what I don't know. But I cannot be the only person responsible for learning and understanding someone. Knowing and learning about your friends, their hardships, and what drives them is important too. We all have experienced trauma or difficulties of some sort.

I never meant to hurt you. I want you to know that I love you and I wish you the best. You will always have a special place in my heart. I hope we reconnect at some point in this life or the next.

Xo

12

It is time to let go

I never heard back from Alan. A week after I responded to his email, I panicked. I realized that it was actually over. I needed reassurance and didn't really have anyone to talk to that would give it to me. So, I decided to see a psychic, desperately hoping for answers, a soothsayer to provide light to my dark future. I needed someone to ease the feelings boiling up inside me— hurt, pain, loss—all emotions that I could not suppress. These feelings weighed heavily; they conquered me and imprisoned me in an airtight vault, desperate for air. I could not breathe. I wanted to be released. This state of being had to be temporary; I wanted to be told that things would settle down in two weeks or a month, and we'd resume our lives as they were. I needed the fantasy, longed for it, and wanted someone to validate it and give it to me. Only then could I get to a place where peace of mind resided.

Now, I hear the door open behind me and I quickly wipe my eyes. Elena enters the room, lights another incense stick, and sits across from me. She notices my eyes are red and promptly apologizes for her absence. She clears her throat, closes her eyes, grabs my hands, and begins the session.

An hour later, I leave the psychic's office and head back out into the sunshine. Unfortunately, my meeting with the psychic provided no reprieve. She said that I had a demon clouding my path, and I needed to be treated to dispel it. I would need to meet with her twice a month, a hundred dollars per session. She would do prayers and recommend foods and spices to eat. Only then would my demon be exorcised, and my life would go back as it was, as I wanted it to be. Her offer tempted me, but I knew the monster I struggled with was within.

Kenji is graciously allowing me to stay at his apartment in Jersey City. After staying in the hotel for about two weeks, I move in with him. I reach out to Jacob at this time. I need to get some of my things from his apartment, but I also want to check in with him. I miss him, which surprises me. When I decided to leave him for Alan, I was sure I was making the right decision. My feelings were so strong on the matter, but now, I'm unsure of everything that's happened and in a different state of mind. Plus, I want to see if he's okay, so I text him.

Hey, I'm probably the last person you want to hear from. I just wanted to check in and see how you're doing?

Within minutes, Jacob responds. *I'm not great. I'm still in shock about how you left, with no real explanation for why. I'm not only shocked but hurt.*

My heart sinks. I never did explain to him why I ran out—I just ran out. I turned my back on someone who showed me he loved me every day.

I'm sorry. You didn't deserve to be treated the way I treated you. Is it possible for us to speak in person? I need to come over to get a few things and would appreciate the opportunity for us to speak. I type the message, read it twice, and hit send. An hour passes by before I receive his message.

Yes, I'm available. Can you do this Wednesday evening?

Going back to the apartment, I feel like a stranger, even though it was a home that we lived in together for four years. I have a key, but I choose to knock. One knock, two knocks, and I wait. The door opens, and Jacob stands there in the frame. At that moment, I realize that I want my old life back; I want him back. He was my home, my place of retreat, my refuge. However, it feels too late to explain this epiphany, especially given our current affairs. Seeing him with his dark brown eyes and olive skin brings joy but also an overwhelming sense of guilt. I am face to face with someone whom I loved and who loved me, but I realize that I broke us apart and am the cause of deep disappointment. I feel incapacitated, unable to speak or move. Jacob is the first to speak.

"Come inside. Can I get you anything? Water or something hot—coffee?"

"Maybe a water?" I say, regaining my senses.

Jacob grabs a glass of water for me, and we sit on the velvet green sofa we had bought together at a furniture store on a weekend outing in Williamsburg. There is minimal small talk. He asks about my job, and I do the same regarding his. Then we go into the purpose of my visit, which is to explain my actions.

I come clean about Alan, the trip, what happened, and the feelings I thought I had developed for Alan over three years. We talk for hours. He asks how long it had been going on, details about our encounters, why I thought I loved Alan, and why I was willing to dispose of our relationship to pursue one with him. I have a hard time answering the last question. The "why"—why was it so easy to let go of a relationship with someone who truly loved me, who showed up and supported me in all aspects of my life? I have no words to justify my actions; I simply say, "I don't know."

But that isn't enough for Jacob. He makes it clear that he deserves more. Jacob spent years cultivating his sense of self; he refuses to allow himself to accept anything less than what he believes he deserves, which is, as he states, love and mutual trust. To my surprise, Jacob softens and says, "I still love you. The door isn't closed. But you've hurt me tremendously."

Instantly, I respond, "I love you too. I'm sorry. I don't know what's wrong with me. I feel so broken, like there's no way love could be so easy." I am barely able to get the words out as I drown in my tears and my body seizes.

"Eddie, love isn't easy. It takes work. I've worked to build trust with you. It pains me to know that you didn't consider my feelings in all of this. I want to believe that you can, and that you can possibly change, do better."

My actions broke his trust in me, and he needs it to be re-established for our relationship to work. The love is there, but the fundamental cornerstone supporting it is not. I ask him what he needs from me, and he replies, "I need you to work on yourself, start therapy, show me that you're ready to be in a relationship and to love me the way I deserve to be loved. I can't promise that I will be here for you once you reach that state, but I still love you. For now, I need time to heal. If we do get back into a relationship, I need you to be able to share what it is you need to feel loved. Most importantly, I need to know that I can trust you again."

***

My therapist's office is in her home in Bed-Stuy, a brownstone on Jefferson Avenue near the Tompkins Avenue commercial corridor. I walk up the steps, nervous—unsure what to expect. In my family, and for most Nigerian families I know, no one goes to therapy. Sharing your deepest and darkest thoughts and feelings with strangers is considered a sign of weakness. I think my mother may have discouraged me if I told her I'm starting treatment. I imagine her saying, "You don't need therapy! Why? Isn't that for crazy people or something only white people do?" The fact is that doing what I'd been brought up to do isn't working. I need to try something new.

I ring the doorbell, and within a minute, a thirty-something black woman with shoulder-length locs dressed in gender-neutral clothing appears. Her presence instantly calms me. "Hello, Eddie, welcome. I'm Ada; please come in." Her voice is soothing, deepened by the richness of her accent. She is British, with family ties to Nigeria. Jacob recommended her as a person I should consider talking to.

She leads me to her front room parlor. The white walls reflect the sun's rays, which flood the room. There is a largescale, high-definition colorful image of an older African woman adorned with beads and shells hanging above her mahogany fireplace mantle accented by shimmery green tile. On the opposite wall is a bookcase filled with books. The furniture is placed in the middle of the room. Her home has the faint smell of cinnamon. She directs me to sit or lie on the couch, and she takes her place on the chair. I choose to sit.

"Eddie, I approach therapy as a collaborative process built on exploration and understanding. In our work together, there is potential for realization and creative resolution to occur when we both show up courageously and honestly during our sessions. I want you to feel comfortable during our sessions. This is a safe space. How does that sound to you?"

"It sounds good," I say, feeling at ease by her voice and overall presence.

"What is it that you want to talk about, Eddie?"

"I'm here because I don't know how to make myself feel better. I recently ended a friendship that has left me feeling empty inside. I feel lost, maybe even depressed. I don't want to feel this way anymore. I want to get better. I need you to help me get better."

"Eddie, unfortunately, I can't make you feel better. But I can help you understand why you feel lost. What if you allowed yourself to sit with the feeling of loss? What comes up for you?"

"I feel rejected, dismissed, and unwanted. It hurts," I say, feeling my eyelids get heavy as tears fill them to the rim.

"What part of you feels rejected?"

"The parts of value. My body, mind, and heart; my very identity. I couldn't give him what he needed."

"Give who? And what exactly?"

"Alan." The tears spill onto my face.

"Eddie, it isn't your job to give someone what they need. We are responsible for ensuring that our needs are met first. In relationships with others, you don't have to be more than who you are to be considered enough. You are enough."

"But I don't feel that way." My voice becomes small, something I was used to in moments when I found myself unsure.

"Eddie, I want you to try something. Why don't you lie down and close your eyes? I want you to envision an older version of yourself. This version has all the traits and characteristics you feel will make you enough. Hold that vision in your mind for a few minutes... Now, can you share what you saw?"

"I saw someone who was confident, smart, and had a sense of purpose. Someone who was happy, who people respected and liked to be around."

"Eddie, why don't you believe you possess those traits now?"

"I've just never felt that way about myself."

"Can you share why?"

And, from there, a current of words flow. I share. I share stories about my childhood. I confide in her about confusing the word Niger for nigger while reading out loud. About my insecurity around making friends, especially with the white boys in my class growing up, about passing out candy to get people to like me, about hiding my sexuality, about my uneasiness about being black, about my general desire to be good enough, to be liked. Ada listens; I can sense her body leaning forward as my eyes remain locked on the moving ceiling fan. I am too afraid to look at her as I share my secrets. For forty-five minutes, I talk without censoring myself, letting the words flow; a stream building momentum and finally surging down the rocky cliff, unblocked by the dam I had constructed over time.

"Eddie, we are out of time. You've done a lot of work today. You've done some heavy lifting, uncovering things in your past that have caused you pain. It is never comfortable unveiling past trauma, nor is it easy to identify areas that elicit feelings of shame. During our next session, I'd like to discuss this in more depth with you, but I want to leave you with this. Shame is what happens when our most basic needs are left unmet. You wanted to be accepted for who you are but received messaging that it was not enough, and so you tried to be what others wanted you to be—which only reinforced this belief of inadequacy.

"As a consequence, you've accepted a false reality; that you are not good enough. You've chosen to avoid anything contrary to this belief. Eddie, avoidance doesn't heal. It can only provide a false sense of safety. To heal, we must understand the root cause of our pain and allow ourselves to feel it, carry it, and show it a new path. Together, we will work to care for that younger version of yourself who believes he's not enough and help him understand that he is."

***

I will continue to see Ada, will start building my emotional intelligence and fortitude—and will learn to communicate my needs to family, friends, and my loved one, Jacob. Slowly, slowly, I will confront my shame. The shame that the ten-year-old version of myself held on to and brought up for me during times of strife. I will understand that my inner child was afraid and wanted to protect me from the pain of feeling inadequate and being rejected by others. However, I will start to confront my fears. I will take my inner child and introduce him to the older, wiser version of myself. All three of us will walk together and find inner peace.

13

Epilogue

And so, the work began. Within a year, Eddie was on a clear path to emotional stability. Eddie made peace with losing his friendship with Alan and embarked on a trajectory towards inner peace. He took back the energy spent ruminating on Alan and reinvested it into himself and those who nurtured his internal growth. Eddie sought healing. With the help of his therapist, he went on an investigation into his deepest parts. Through discovery, Eddie found clues that provided context for his behavior, exploring the destructive choices he made that led him to Alan and away from Jacob.

The relationship between Eddie and Jacob went through a metamorphosis. For the first time, it was tested. Amid Eddie's exploration, Jacob undertook his own journey to seek understanding. He demanded to understand the "why." Why would his partner of six years betray him in a way that brought harm to him and their relationship? He, of course, understood that Eddie's actions were not a reflection of him or a testament to his inability to love. Still, this experience hurt him deeply. It also taught him a lesson, which was the importance for him to clearly articulate his own needs and maintain a vocabulary, complete with diverse adjectives and verbs, that described how he wanted to be loved. Jabob's heart was worthy of protection too, and this was a fact he communicated to Eddie, who had to confront and acknowledge this on his road back to him.

Ultimately, Jacob decided to forgive Eddie and move forward in their relationship. Together, they rebuilt organizing principles established on intimacy, trust, and communication. Eddie earnestly worked to show progress in these areas, sharing with Jacob every precious stone uncovered with all its facets. It took six months for this to happen. During that time, Jacob lived with Kenji. However, eventually, after that period, they moved back in together. They both continued to relearn, reexamine, and devote themselves to each other, breaking new ground in the process, both contributing and rebuilding a foundation built to last.

***

Alan landed the job in Denver. It had all the trappings he'd hoped for: six figures, mid-management, and a portfolio of projects without day-to-day oversight. In September, six months after his relationship with Eddie ended, David came to New York to help Alan pack up his life and drive cross-country to Colorado. During the period between the offer letter and the move, Alan decided he just wanted to have fun and forget about everything, indulging in all the city had to offer, with a hyper-focus on dating. Alan treated dating like a job, poring over profiles for compatibility, expertly answering the screening questions to land in-person meetings, and while capturing their attention, doing his best to seal the deal by the first date.

When Alan finally left New York, he felt satisfied. He'd done everything he set out to do and was ready for a new adventure. On the road, the conversation between Alan and David vacillated between the past, the present, and their dreams for the future. Amid their reflections, David asked about Eddie. "How's Eddie, by the way? You don't talk about him anymore."

The question caught Alan off guard. He felt his body react, a tinge along his neck, an aching sensation. He quickly straightened up and said, "I don't know, we fell out."

"Oh, really. Over what?"

Alan paused, looking out the window as David drove, and plainly said, "Nothing important." Alan decided to push forward, allowing memories of Eddie and their time together to decompose within a casket, along with all the others he locked within.

About the Author

Anthony Amiewalan is the author of *Eddie & Alan*, his debut novel. Before writing *Eddie & Alan*, Anthony published *Jojoba* a memoir and a book of illustrations, *A Visual Diary*. He is based in Brooklyn, New York, with his husband Dean Estrada.

Milton Keynes UK
Ingram Content Group UK Ltd.
UKHW010814100324
439004UK00003B/29